Swamp Jesus

Scott Parish

This book is dedicated to my favorite guitar picker and the
kindest soul I have had the honor to meet.
It happens that they are brothers.

To Brandon "Cotton" Clifton and the eternal memory of
Madison James Clifton

About This Book

Several years ago, I lived in a town in West Tennessee. It was my hometown. I was involved in the bar business on many levels, the greatest being drinking. It was quite a party. One that my brother, Jeremy, and I shared practically every day. That great adventure led me to meet two brothers who had recently relocated from Louisiana. I learned later from Madison that I was the first person they met from Jackson, and as fate would have it, I was a good connection to introduce these brothers to the local music scene. Also, despite the gap in years between the boys and me, we found a solid friendship that weathered some storms and celebrated some victories. They were good days.

We lost Madison along the way to overdose, and I hope, as my memory fades, I will never forget the last time he and I talked on the phone. We were discussing how we could get his true love and him down to my new home in Florida for a visit.

Brandon, a powerful personality who lights the stage with his presence and is an even louder defender of injustice, is continuing to make his mark on the world. He has a way when offering to share stories over a cold can of PBR or relating historical details of country and folk music that capture the spirit of Americana. You will never leave disappointed.

During a few late nights at the Downtown Tavern after Brandon began growing his beard to hairy obscenity, someone began teasing him by calling him Swamp Jesus as a nod to his bayou birth. I knew there was a story somewhere in there, and one day I would tell it.

While this story is completely fiction, it did give me an opportunity to recognize a few people through characterization, name, and original lyrics. There are the obvious ones for Jackson and Paducah folk. I look forward to seeing who identifies the rest. BUT don't ask me. I share this tale for your entertainment and consideration.

Chapter One

Dillon sat on the back of Greg's black '92 four-door Impala. School had never been his thing. He'd skipped the last period; he had no interest in who the forefathers were or whatever they were discussing in civics class. When was that ever going to land him a paying gig?

His long, dishwater-blonde hair fell past his shoulders. His jeans were worn, and his T-shirt sported a rock band name under a crudely drawn happy face emblem. He looked up at the afternoon Louisiana sun. Summer was on its way, and the heat would follow. This was Dillon's favorite time of year. The days were getting longer, though the pine forests still clung to signs of spring.

Other teenagers passed by in ones, twos, and threes. Some were lost in their cliquish conversations. Others waved or gave Dillon a head nod as they walked past. He glanced toward the school at the end of the parking lot. The stream of students thickened as the building emptied.

Greg approached the car with a burst of energy. He and Dillon couldn't have looked more different. Greg's six-three, two-thirty frame dwarfed Dillon's five-ten, one-sixty. Greg liked to joke that he only weighed "a hundred and four kilos in Europe" because it sounded lighter. Dillon got the joke, though places that used metric measurements might as well have been on another planet.

Greg knew things; he'd experienced a life Dillon couldn't imagine. His jeans were crisply creased, and his black golf shirt had a logo from some far-off course Dillon had never heard of. Greg's short, curly hair was always neat, and his wire-rimmed glasses completed the look of a middle-aged accountant more than that of an eighteen-year-old high school student.

Then there was his smile. It wasn't a put-on. Greg's smile was constant and contagious. Dillon even thought, fleetingly, that Greg would make a great Santa Claus one day at family gatherings, surrounded by adoring kids and grown-ups alike.

Greg didn't seem to mind. That approachable, adult vibe he gave off meant he was rarely carded when buying alcohol, something he took full advantage of at the local ABC store.

"What's up, dork?" Greg said, slapping Dillon on the shoulder.

Dillon smiled at his friend and answered, "What it be, dog? Let's blow this popsicle stand."

The steady stream of kids was briefly interrupted as Dillon slid from his perch to his feet. Two girls stopped directly in front of him, both casting coy glances his way. Their interest in him was obvious.

One asked, "Are you playing at the Swamp tonight?"

Dillon smiled. "Our first set starts around nine."

"I got a new fake ID," she said. Then, with an exaggerated turn, she looked back at Dillon flirtatiously. "We'll be ready to party."

As the girls walked off, Dillon gave a simple "Yeah" and a nod in her direction.

He rounded the car to the passenger side as Greg moved to the driver's door. Greg paused before getting in, placing a hand under his chin and stroking it in mock thought. "You know, I think I need a pair of girls like that. Life goals…"

Dillon laughed as he got into the car. "You're a dork."

Greg climbed in, started the engine, and pulled out onto the road in front of the school.

They left the school parking lot and drove along a road that led out of town. The city gave way to fields dotted with pine trees. Gravel roads intersected the pavement at regular intervals until eventually, the paved road itself turned to gravel. The car kicked up long dusty plumes as buildings grew scarcer. In the distance, they finally saw a lone single-wide trailer at the edge of a field. It stood like a forgotten beacon to lost travelers, a landmark that was neither welcoming nor warm, like a strange rock jutting from the shoreline of a far-off ocean.

As they approached, the trailer looked even less inviting. It's a dirty brown film clinging to an off-white exterior. The field around it seemed to be reclaiming the land, with weeds overtaking the trailer inch by inch. A once-red Ford Ranger, now faded and scratched, was parked near the weathered wooden steps that led to the front door. The truck bed was piled with what most would call junk, all of it blanketed in dust.

Greg pulled the car into the yard beside the truck and shifted into park.

"I'll be right back," Dillon said as he opened the car door.

As he stepped out, he noticed the driver's side window was down, and the inside of the cab was just as filthy as the exterior. He shook his head at the lack of thought it took to leave the window open, then headed up the stairs and into the house.

The thought crossed his mind, one day he would leave. He was torn, and a little afraid of what the world outside this bubble might hold.

Inside, the house was dim, an abrupt contrast to the bright sunlight outside. Weak sunlight slipped through thin, threadbare curtains. A single floor lamp, half-hidden behind a worn recliner, gave the room just enough light to see.

Devon, pronounced DEE-von, sat slouched in the recliner with a tray balanced on his lap, rolling a joint while blankly watching a game show across the room. He was Dillon's mom's latest live-in boyfriend.

Maybe all of them had been live-ins, or more accurately, squatters. Dillon could barely remember most of their names. They all looked the same: tired, aimless copies of whoever came before. His mom always seemed to attract guys with no ambition, a welfare check, and a desperate need for somewhere to crash. That place was always Denise's house.

Devon didn't even glance at Dillon as he walked in, and Dillon returned the favor. Devon had made it clear: Dillon was just dead weight in his relationship with Denise. He'd muttered more than once that life would be easier without "some damn kid" hanging around.

"MOM!" Dillon called into the house.

"Back here, honey," came her reply from the open bathroom door.

Dillon walked toward the sound of his mother's voice. She was a wisp of a person, so light, a gentle breeze could have taken her away. She sat cross-legged on the bathroom vanity, facing the mirror. Under the harsh glow of a bare bulb mounted above the sink, she leaned in carefully to apply eyeliner. Her overly bleached, thinning hair fell to the middle of her back. Her bird-like arms bore old needle tracks on weathered skin. The makeup couldn't hide the hard life she had lived, yet her eyes sparkled when she saw her son. She looked up and caught his reflection in the mirror, her cigarette-stained smile showing genuine love.

"How was school?" she asked.

Dillon looked at the floor, shrugged, and said, "I don't know."

He knew she didn't care. The only time he could remember her being involved with school was back in eighth grade during Parents' Day. She had shown up high as a three-story building and left a cigarette butt in the store-bought cookies she'd brought.

Denise lowered her hands into her lap and said, "Well, you're almost out of there. Today was the last day, right?"

She lifted her beauty tools back to her face as he answered, "Yes."

"Are you playing tonight?" she asked. She didn't wait for a response. "Devon and I are having date night. Steaks on the grill. He got his check today. And beer only, no whiskey, so no fights."

Denise paused and looked at Dillon's reflection in the mirror again. She smiled.

"You know," she continued, "I remember graduating from high school. I was seven months preggers with you."

She stopped for a moment, her face slipping into a faraway look.

"Your dad did such a good job taking care of me," she said. "I miss him so much."

Dillon watched her reflection. The shared pang of loss touched his heart.

"I know, Mom," he said.

Dillon broke the moment by turning toward his room, which was wedged between the bathroom and the living room. Two steps and he was in the doorway. The bed was unmade and took up most of the space. A mirrored dresser dominated one wall and nearly all of the remaining floor area. Clothes were scattered around in indistinguishable piles of clean and dirty.

Dillon walked over to the dresser, opened and closed a couple of drawers, then scanned the room until his eyes settled on one pile. He pulled a western-style plaid shirt with pearl-colored buttons from the stack. Stripping off his t-shirt, he tossed it into the same pile and put on the button-up shirt. He ran his hands down the front in a feeble attempt to smooth the wrinkles. Then he picked up his guitar case, ready to leave.

"HONEY," came his mother's voice.

He followed it back to the bathroom, where she was still seated.

"Give Momma a kiss," she requested, turning toward him.

Dillon gave her a peck on the cheek and paused, looking at her for a long moment. She deserved a better life than this one. Maybe one day, he could give that to her.

He turned toward the front door and headed out.

"Love you too. Be careful tonight," Denise called after his vanishing figure.

Once outside, Dillon slid his guitar into the backseat and reclaimed his place in the passenger seat beside Greg.

"Let's get out of here," he said.

Greg started the car, bumping through the rutted yard before steering toward his own house.

The drive was short. Greg lived closer to town. All the yards in his neighborhood were neatly manicured, and the mailboxes stood in uniform rows, identical boxes on identical posts at the end of each driveway. His family's home looked just like the others around it. A clean, shiny bass boat sat to the side of the double-car garage.

Greg pulled into the empty driveway and parked. He and Dillon got out and walked to the front door. Dillon had been here countless times, but every time he stepped inside, it felt like entering another world.

The living room was filled with large, overstuffed furniture, tastefully chosen and neatly arranged. Dillon paused to take in the forty-two-inch flat-screen TV mounted on the wall. Greg's family was the only one he knew who owned one. Framed photos of Greg and his parents were everywhere, showing the three of them on boats, skis, beaches, and in cities. Dillon liked being in this room.

It felt... safe.

Greg's mom entered from the breakfast nook that connected the kitchen to the living area.

"Boys," she greeted them with a warm smile.

She wore a conservative skirt and a smart blouse. Dillon thought she always dressed like she could be coming from a boardroom meeting or a library book club. Not a single thread or hair on her head was ever out of place. She moved with smooth, effortless confidence. Dillon guessed she was in her mid-forties, though she was in excellent shape.

"Hey, Mom," Greg said. "Is Dad home yet?"

"No, dear," she replied. "He's on a business trip and will be home tomorrow."

"Would you two like some dinner?" she asked.

"Yes, ma'am," Dillon answered enthusiastically.

"Dang," Greg laughed. "Give this boy some food, I think he's starving."

"Well," his mom said, "that's certainly something we can fix. Go wash your hands and have a seat at the table."

The boys did as they were told. Once they were seated, Greg's mom placed heaping bowls of steaming jambalaya in front of them.

"This is my mother's recipe," she said. "I expect you'll like it."

Greg and Dillon dug in greedily as she watched. Dillon paused long enough to say, "This is delicious," which brought a smile to her face.

She moved around the table and took a seat in an empty chair, resting her forearms on the table. For a few moments, she just watched them eat.

Then she broke the silence. "Do you have all your paperwork together that Vandy requested?"

Greg leaned back in his chair, taking a break from his meal.

"Yes, ma'am. I mailed the package to them yesterday."

"What's Vandy?" Dillon asked coyly.

"This college in Nashville," Greg explained. "My parents went there. In fact it's where they met. I guess that makes me a legacy or something, so that's where I'm going. My dad wants me to go into accounting like him."

"What do you think?" Dillon asked.

Greg looked thoughtfully at his plate before answering. "I think I want to be a rodeo clown."

His mom slapped him playfully on the arm as they all burst into laughter. "You do not," she added, still laughing at the absurdity.

"What about you, Dillon?" Greg's mom asked. "Have you made plans for where you want to go to school?"

Dillon froze and looked down at the table, unable to make eye contact.

"No. I think I'm going to find a job and maybe go later," he said.

His eyes drifted to hers. He could see the pity she felt for him. He felt a pang of regret. He didn't have the grades or resources to go to college. He wouldn't even know where to start if he did want to go. The only thing he knew he could do well was play guitar. He didn't know how, but music was his only choice, and that might never get him past the edge of town.

"I understand," she told him. "That's a good plan, too."

The two young men finished their dinner. Greg's mom rose from her seat and took the empty bowls into the kitchen.

"Come on," Greg said as he stood. "Let's go to my room."

Dillon followed Greg. Greg's room was three times the size of Dillon's. Greg's Eagle Scout badge hung in a shadowbox on the wall. Dillon stopped to examine it for the millionth time. "Be prepared" was emblazoned on the tiny banner above the eagle.

Dillon only felt prepared when he was performing on stage. That was the place he could control. He sometimes wondered what it was like for Greg, where everything seemed to fall into place. Dillon wasn't jealous. He was proud of his friend, the straight-A student, class secretary, voted "Funniest Student."

Dillon looked around the room. Books, trophies, and souvenirs adorned the shelves and side tables. A set of golf clubs leaned against one corner. Cleated shoes rested at the base of the bag. A smaller version of the flat-screen television from the living room sat on the dresser at the end of Greg's bed.

Dillon was lost in thought, imagining a world where he lived like Greg's family.

Greg dropped onto the end of his bed and picked up a game controller.

"Come on, man," he jeered. "Grab the other controller so I can school you."

Dillon laughed as he sat beside Greg with the second controller.

"You're a dumbass," he said.

But Dillon couldn't keep his focus on the game. He had retrieved his guitar from Greg's car earlier, and now he sat plucking at the strings, barely watching the screen. As Greg maneuvered the avatar, Dillon observed him, thinking how much Greg resembled the fearless, dominating character on screen.

I wonder if I could be like that... maybe, if it had something to do with music, he thought.

The idea brought him an odd sense of comfort.

Tonight is going to be a good night.

Greg and Dillon arrived at The Swamp not long after dark. The parking lot was just packed dirt, connecting the main road to the run-down building. A weathered sign on the roof marked the bar's name, and the place itself was a squat structure of wood and cinder blocks. Thick, aged logs framed the porch, and the heavy black metal door was propped open, welcoming anyone willing to step inside.

A short Hispanic man sat on a stool by the door, checking IDs. His long hair was tied into a ponytail that reached his waist. His jeans were stained but fit well with his work boots and biker jacket over a plain black tee. He might've looked intimidating, if not for the mischievous glint that never seemed to leave his eyes.

"¡Hola, boys!" he called as Greg and Dillon got out of the car and headed over.

"Julio!" Greg responded, pulling him into a quick hug and a backslap. "What's happening, my dog?"

Julio grinned. "Ah, you know, just living the dream. Or the nightmare, depending on how you look at it."

Dillon bumped fists with him.

"How's the crowd looking so far?" he asked.

"It's going to be a big night. Hope you're ready, amigo," Julio said with a wink. "Arthur said to find him when you get here."

"Heard," Dillon replied as he and Greg walked past him and into the bar.

Inside, the lighting was dim except for the glow behind the bar and a few strands of Christmas lights randomly draped across the ceiling. Greg made his way over to the bartender, while Dillon headed toward the stage near the back of the room.

Equipment was scattered across the platform. An elderly Black man sat in a chair from one of the nearby tables, focused solely on the sleek, wood-grain guitar in his lap. The ivory pickups gleamed as he tuned and polished them. His hands trembled slightly, and Dillon noticed the familiar shake.

He'd seen that twitch before.

How did Arthur put it?

Only a little scratch could fix some itches.

Dillon stepped onto the stage and greeted the old man.

"Arthur! What's happening?"

It was always hard for Dillon to explain his relationship with Arthur; it went deeper than the music. Sure, Arthur was a mentor. But he was more than that. A broken Vietnam vet who'd come home with no prospects and a monkey on his back, Arthur had managed to carve out a space in a world full of pain and burden. He reminded Dillon that the battles inside could be harder than the ones outside. But that never gave you a reason to quit. In that way, Arthur gave Dillon hope.

Dillon tried to remember when they first met. Maybe when he was ten.

Denise had taken him to a third-rate drug dealer's house to score. She sat him on a stained couch in the living room while she disappeared into the back. Arthur had been sitting on the other end of the couch.

At first, they both pretended the other didn't exist. Minutes passed. Then Arthur broke the silence.

"What's your name, boy?"

Dillon answered softly. His mom had told him never to talk to anyone, no matter what. He glanced at Arthur without turning his head, what he called a side eye. Arthur must've noticed.

"You want to learn something?" Arthur asked.

Dillon shifted on the couch so he could look at him directly, still quiet but paying attention. Arthur picked up a beat-up guitar leaning against the wall and placed it in Dillon's hands. He guided Dillon's fingers into position. Dillon had to strain to keep them there. Then he dragged his other hand across the strings and smiled.

"That's a G," Arthur said. "Not a good one, but a G all the same. Let me show you another chord."

Dillon was pretty sure that was the moment he fell in love with music.

It became the first of many visits Denise made to that house with Dillon in tow. Before long, Arthur was teaching him regularly. And on his twelfth birthday, Arthur gave him his first guitar.

Arthur's voice pulled Dillon back to the present.

"Hello, young man. You ready to play tonight?"

Dillon grinned. "For sure. We're gonna jam."

Arthur nodded, then got serious.

"I want to talk about that new song we added to the set. You did pretty well, but tonight I want you to play with intention. Let it go where it wants. Then stop. Leave space."

His voice rose.

"No, create space. Let your sound blend."

"For sure," Dillon said, upbeat. "I got this."

Arthur went back to wiping down the guitar with a cloth and smiled.

"I know you do, young man. Yes, you do."

Dillon stepped past Arthur and picked up an electro-acoustic guitar resting on a stand on the stage. He plugged it into an amp, tuned it, and strummed its chords. As he fingered the strings, he thought about the songs and the order they'd be played tonight. The other band members filtered onto the stage and took their places. Arthur remained in his chair, shifting slightly to play from where he sat. The stage lights dimmed. Dillon stepped up to the microphone.

This was where he felt whole, like everything made sense.

He gazed out over the small crowd seated at tables, all eyes on him. Whether it was ten people or ten thousand, he didn't care. He just wanted to play.

Leaning into the microphone, Dillon announced, "Thank y'all for coming tonight. We are The Bayou Hunters Band, and we are ready to PAR-TEE! Who's with me?"

A lone "whoop" came from Greg near the bar, but the rest of the patrons remained indifferent. Dillon glanced back at the band and caught Arthur's eye. Arthur gave a nod and coaxed a long, soulful whine from his guitar just as Dillon turned back to the mic and began to sing.

People trickled into the bar. Some watched the band. Others milled around, more focused on drinking. As time passed, the crowd swelled. Tables were pushed aside to make space for dancing. Rowdy backwoods patrons shouted, laughed, argued, and drank. Whiskey and cheap beer flowed steadily from the bar.

Dillon and the band played louder, urging the crowd to let loose. A few girls pressed up to the front of the stage, dancing provocatively in hopes of catching Dillon's attention. He smiled appreciatively as he was entertained by the spotlight.

One particularly striking blonde flirted as best she could from the foot of the stage. Dillon figured she was at least ten years older than he, maybe more. But with that tight skirt and half-open blouse, age stopped mattering. From the moment he started playing, he could tell she was hooked.

He knew if they'd crossed paths on a sidewalk downtown in broad daylight, she wouldn't have given him a second glance. But up here, in his element, everything was different. This was his world. He sang to her directly:

"If there's anything at all that's wrong with her

It's something I just can't see

Ain't no doubt about me

She's the same kind of crazy as me."

The band wrapped up their set. Dillon slipped the guitar strap from around his neck and leaned the guitar against a stand. He was sweating, elated by how well the night had gone. For the first time that evening, Arthur stood from his chair.

Dillon asked, "What do you think? Pretty damn good, huh?"

Arthur looked him over and replied evenly, "You did all right, young man. Let's get together tomorrow and talk about some key changes."

Dillon grinned widely. "You got it, old man. Let me buy you a drink."

Arthur shook his head. "No thanks. I've got to take a piss anyway."

He headed toward the bathroom. Dillon spotted Greg and joined him at the bar.

"Shot of tequila," Dillon said in a loud, confident voice.

The bartender leaned across the gap between them and spoke low. "You know as well as I do, it's legal for you to play in here at eighteen, but drinking's out of the question. Don't go risking my liquor license."

Greg, his face lit with the flush of drunkenness, laughed and clapped Dillon on the shoulder. Dillon rolled his eyes dramatically and made his way to the bathroom.

The door was flimsy and swung wide open when Dillon pushed it. The bathroom was dingy and cramped, divided into three open stalls, two with toilets, one with a sink and a mirror made of polished metal.

Arthur sat on one of the toilets with a kit in his lap and an IV needle poised in one hand, ready to tap a vein in the other. He looked up calmly and said, "Watch that door for a minute. Don't need any more unexpected guests."

Dillon's heart sank at the sight, though it wasn't the first time. He drew in a breath, trying to mask his disappointment, and leaned against the door to block it from opening.

Arthur continued, calm as if he were tying his shoes. Once the needle was in, he closed his eyes and sighed.

Dillon thought, I hate how normal this feels.

"Okay, old man," Dillon urged. "I gotta go. Get your ass up."

Arthur folded his kit, stood, and spat some vomit into the toilet. Then he turned and, for the first time that night, smiled.

"Mais, boy," Arthur said, "watch yourself. I'll have to fold you up like a fifth-grade love letter."

Dillon smirked. "Yeah, I know. Now let me piss already."

Arthur sauntered out of the bathroom, and Dillon stepped up to the urinal.

Chapter Two

The summer passed as most Louisiana summers do, lazy and hot. The sun beat down on the fields and forests. Heat shimmered off the streets of the small town that Dillon called home.

Dillon and Greg sat in Greg's car in a convenience store parking lot. There's really nothing quite like a Louisiana convenience store. If you sat at one long enough, you'd see everyone in town eventually. Where else could you buy plain white t-shirts, gas, rolling papers, and boudin all in the same place?

They watched the traffic roll by in momentary silence.

"I'm leaving tomorrow. You know that, right?" Greg said.

"Headed for that college in Tennessee?" Dillon asked, trying to sound as uninterested as possible.

Greg kept his eyes on the passing cars. "Yeah. Classes start in a few days. I've got to get settled into the dorm."

"I thought you were getting an apartment."

"No," Greg turned to look at Dillon. A brief flicker of pain crossed his face as he realized he was talking about something his best friend could only imagine. "All freshmen have to stay in what they call 'The Commons.' Dad said I can get my place next year if I keep my grades up."

Dillon stared out the windshield.

Well, hell, he thought. So, this is it. The last time we're probably ever gonna chill like this.

A flash of anger passed through him and quickly burned out.

I get it. Some people catch the breaks, get the good life, the everything. It's not his fault. He was born in the right house. I'm glad he gets to leave. He won't come back. I wouldn't.

Greg had been his anchor, and now that anchor was slipping away. A hollow ache welled up in Dillon. Something inside him was dying, and he couldn't quite put a name to it.

Greg broke the silence. "Let's grab a couple of road drinks. I heard there's a party tonight on Annie Bell Parish Road."

The mention of a party pulled Dillon back to the moment. His despair evaporated, replaced by a spark of excitement.

"Let's do it," he said, almost too fast.

Greg threw the car into drive and pulled out of the lot. A few blocks later, he turned into Shots Fired Drive-Through Drinks. A middle-aged man met them at the window and asked gruffly, "What do you want?"

Greg pulled his wallet from his back pocket and produced a hundred-dollar bill.

He ordered, "Two Walk Me Down Sweet Jesus and a fifth of Crown."

The man at the window scrutinized Dillon. Dillon glanced at Greg, who sat patiently, as if nothing about the situation was out of the ordinary.

Dillon felt a pang at the thought that he would miss how calm and collected Greg could be, no matter the circumstance.

The liquor store clerk rubbed his chin. "I don't know if that other guy's old enough to be drinking. I'm going to need some ID."

Greg smiled and gave the man his best I-know-what-you-mean look. Holding the bill out, he said, "They're both for me. It's been a long day at the office."

The man at the window took the Benjamin and fingered it thoughtfully, eyeing Greg like he was weighing his options. Finally, he folded the bill in half and slid it into his pocket before disappearing into the store. Moments later, he returned with the bottle of whiskey and two large plastic cups filled with drinks.

Greg took the liquor and gave the man a wave as he pulled away.

They drove out into the county, where farms and fields dotted the landscape.

"Do you remember in sixth grade when you liked Sadara Jackson?" Dillon asked.

Greg grinned. "What wasn't to like? She got boobs before anyone else."

Dillon laughed and continued, "You gave her your milk carton at lunch every day and still couldn't talk to her."

"You didn't help!" Greg shot back playfully. "You wrote her that letter. What did it say? I like you more than cake?"

Dillon tried not to laugh. "Well, you like cake. I was trying to be poetic."

"Right," Greg said. "Poetic, and you misspelled cake!"

As they approached a wooded area, Greg turned off the road and followed a grassy path beneath the trees.

Music and raucous laughter drifted in through the open car windows.

Greg drove the car into a shaded glade already occupied by several other cars, haphazardly parked, with clusters of young people milling about in small groups. From the passenger seat, Dillon noticed a guy with a ripped shirt standing in the bed of a pickup truck, playing air guitar to music blasting from a nearby radio. Almost everyone they passed held red Solo cups.

Greg rolled to a stop near a group of people, wearing his best big-politician grin. He raised the cup in his hand out the window in a toast and shouted the unofficial anthem of their graduating class:

"Cajuns, Creole, Coon Asses, Hicks.

Living and partying and getting our kicks.

We are the class of two thousand six!"

The small crowd roared in response, raising their cups and drinking in celebration.

One of the guys, Steve, called out, "We're going down to Booger Holler to race. Y'all in?"

Greg and Dillon exchanged glances. Dillon nodded. Greg turned to the group beside his car and said jokingly, "I don't know if you can keep up with this V8. I'm kind of a bad ass, you know."

The group laughed. Steve stepped forward and replied, "You might have to prove that one. I added a turbocharger and intercooler to my Acura, and I might even have a surprise up my sleeve. Plus, Jamie's got that new Mustang his dad bought him for graduation."

"Well, like Marvin Gaye said to your mom, 'Let's get it on,'" Greg shot back.

The boys whooped and scattered toward their respective cars. Horns blared. Truck beds are filled with people shouting and drinking. Engines roared to life as the cars pulled into a loose parade, leaving the glade.

Greg eased his car into the line behind a truck where two girls and a guy stood in the bed. One of the girls locked eyes with Dillon, set her cup on the roof of the truck, and lifted her shirt, giving him a full view of what lay beneath. Dillon blushed and smiled at her.

Trying to distract himself from the embarrassment, and maybe hold onto the moment a little longer, Dillon spoke up, "Remember when we started calling Steve 'Steve Oh'?"

Greg laughed. "Yeah, it was that one night at the arcade."

Dillon chuckled. "Every time a girl passed by, he'd gawk and say, 'OH!'"

Greg leaned back in his seat and mimicked ecstasy: "Oh... OH... OH! I thought he was gonna lose it right there."

The friends laughed. Then Dillon felt a sudden pang, another moment had passed that he'd never get back.

The line of vehicles continued until they reached a picturesque gravel crossroads. When they stopped, some drivers got out and huddled near the front of the motorcade. Steve barked instructions: "The race will be down Saint Tonis Road to Given's barn, over to Booger Holler Road, and then back here. Any questions?"

Jamie was the first to speak. He leaned against his freshly waxed, meticulously clean hot rod and pushed back his kempt, wavy blond hair. His smug confidence was obvious as he crossed his arms and asked in a cocky tone, "Considering there's no way for any of you to beat me, what do I win?"

Dillon smirked in Jamie's direction. "I've got twenty dollars that says you don't win."

Jamie scoffed and looked away with contempt. "Come on, now. You can do better than that."

Greg appraised the crowd and ran his fingers across the Mustang's fender in mock thought. "Maybe I can. Tell you what, if you don't win, I get your hood emblem. If you do win, I'll give you a hundred bucks."

Anticipation lit up Jamie's eyes. He grinned at Greg. "This is going to be the easiest money I've ever made."

Dillon, still watching the car, nudged Greg. "Trunk emblem."

Greg glanced at him. "What?"

Dillon repeated, "Trunk emblem. It's just held on by a couple of pins, easy to take off. The hood one's a pain."

Greg raised a brow. "How do you know this stuff?"

"With a mom like mine, you learn a lot of things," Dillon shrugged. "Guess it comes in handy."

"Okay," Greg called out, "make that the trunk emblem instead."

Jamie rubbed at a smear on his car that only he could see and taunted, "Whatever. You don't stand a chance, so it doesn't matter."

Greg moved his car into position at the starting line with Dillon riding shotgun. Jamie pulled up beside them.

Steve lined up his Acura, bass-heavy music thumping from the interior. Engines revved. The Acura bounced with the beat. Dillon took a sweeping glance across the line of cars, and the excited crowd gathered to watch. This was a moment he knew would stick with him, no matter what the future held.

One of the girls from the crowd stepped into the middle of the road. She faced the drivers and untied the pink do-rag holding her hair back, raising it like a flag. "On your mark!" she shouted, lifting it high. "Get set," she added, waving it dramatically. "GO!" she screamed as she dropped it.

The three cars lunged forward like hungry animals loosed from a cage. Jamie's Mustang claimed an easy early lead. Greg stayed tight on his tail, the monster engine roaring with power. Steve gave as little room as possible to the bigger cars, watching for an opening to move up.

A few minutes into the race, Dillon pointed excitedly. "The turn into Given's pasture is coming up. There's the barn!"

Greg tightened his grip on the steering wheel and prepared for the sharp turn. Jamie was about a hundred feet ahead, slowing down to make the turn from the gravel road into the cow pasture.

"Hold on, I have a plan!" Greg shouted, hitting the brakes and turning the car into a power slide. A massive cloud of dust engulfed Jamie's car, and rocks sprayed from Greg's spinning tires. He surged into the lead, barely. In the chaos, Steve also passed Jamie.

They neared the barn just as a loud thumping sound from the driver's side drew Greg and Dillon's eyes to the side window. Steve had pulled up beside them, grinning wildly.

"Watch out!" Dillon yelled, just as the Acura slammed into several blue plastic fifty-five-gallon drums stacked beside the barn. Water burst from the barrels, drenching the car and the surrounding field. Dillon twisted in his seat to look back. Steve hadn't stopped. The barrels lay scattered in the aftermath, and though he'd slowed, he hadn't given up.

Greg's car reached the far side of the field first. He eased through the open gate and back onto the gravel road leading to the starting point. Jamie and Steve were close behind.

Jamie pulled up beside Greg, closing the gap. The sun glared on the horizon, and Greg squinted ahead. The finish line loomed. Cheers erupted from the shoulder of the road as Greg floored the accelerator. Jamie's car edged dangerously close on the narrow stretch.

Time seemed to freeze.

A loud honk snapped their attention to the left. Steve's car bounced over every imperfection as he sped along the opposite shoulder, nodding at his rivals. A blue flame flared from his tailpipe, a clear sign he'd been hiding a secret weapon all along. He surged ahead by a full car length.

Greg glanced at Jamie. His brow was furrowed, as if sheer willpower could make the Mustang go faster, but the car had nothing left to give. Greg mashed the accelerator with all his weight, half-wondering if he might drive his foot through the floor.

Dillon braced himself with one hand on the roof and the other on the dashboard as a mix of fear and thrill coursed through him. The cars were maxed out. Steve's Acura, skimming along the side of the road, seemed to leap with excitement as it left the larger machines behind.

Steve looked like a cowboy on a bucking bronco, a wide grin plastered across his face as he clung to the steering wheel, fighting to keep the car on course.

The three cars flashed across the crossroads where the race had begun.

Steve was the clear winner.

The drivers returned to the group of onlookers. Steve laughed and chatted with a bunch of guys gathered around his car. He proudly showed off the nitrous oxide tank mounted in the trunk of the Acura. Giving them a mini tour, he pointed to the switch between the seats and the cable running back to the trunk. Then he popped the hood and kept the tour going. Steve soaked in the group's praise like it was fuel.

Greg made his way over and congratulated him, handing over a crisp hundred-dollar bill. Steve held the note high above his head and presented it to the crowd surrounding his car like it was a trophy.

Jamie exploded. He pointed at Greg and yelled, "This isn't fair! Steve cheated. This is complete crap. Plus, the bet was between YOU AND ME."

Greg raised his hands to calm him down. "It's okay. No one wins every time. No need to get your panties in a wad."

Jamie seethed. "I NEVER lose. This is Steve's fault, maybe yours too. Let's go again. Just you and me. I'll show you."

Quietly, Dillon walked to the back of Jamie's car. Using the flat side of his pocketknife, he popped the trunk emblem off and walked it over to Greg like it was nothing. Greg laughed loud and deep. He held up the emblem, flipping it over a couple of times like he was inspecting it, and said, "Well, fact is, you didn't win, and that was the bet."

Jamie looked like he might cry. He shoved past the kids near his car, yanked open the door, and dropped heavily into the driver's seat. The Mustang roared to life. The crowd stepped back to give him room. Then, in a flurry of dirt and grass, he was gone.

Dillon and Greg watched him drive away. Dillon shook his head. "He's always been like that. I remember in third grade when he threw a tantrum on the ground during Field Day."

Greg grinned. "At least this time he didn't get his jeans dirty."

Chapter Three

THE FOLLOWING YEAR PASSED slowly for Dillon, but he settled into a comfortable routine.

He started driving the Devons' truck, helping his mother hunt for items they could resell. Their finds came from thrift stores, yard sales, or just as often, from piles of discarded belongings on the curb.

On weekends, Dillon played at The Swamp.

One day, as he was driving with his mother in the passenger seat, she suddenly shouted, "STOP!"

She leapt from the truck the moment it came to a halt and began rummaging through a heap of worn and broken furniture on the curb. Dillon guessed it was the aftermath of an eviction, or maybe leftovers from a rental property renovation.

He climbed onto the truck's tailgate and watched her pick through the jumble of clothes, furniture, and knick-knacks. She worked methodically, creating a pile of "keepers" while tossing aside the rest.

"Mom," he asked as she sorted, "what did you want to be when you were young?"

Denise paused, glancing back at him. "When I was young? Honey, I'm not old. What are you asking?"

Dillon felt a pang of guilt. He fidgeted, staring at his hands for a moment before gathering the courage to clarify.

"I mean... did you ever want a career? Or to leave town or something?"

She straightened up, hands on her hips, and gave him a thoughtful look. "Sure, honey. I wanted to be a hairdresser. I dreamed of going to California, just to see if it looked like it does in the movies. Is that what you mean?"

Dillon nodded, then asked softly, "Why didn't you?"

Sadness flickered across Denise's face. Her eyes lost focus as memories surfaced, memories that no one else could see. After a moment, she looked at Dillon. That same loving expression returned, the one she always gave when she truly saw him. Her voice was cracked, touched with melancholy.

"You know, life has a way of slipping past you. Beauty school costs money, and I got pregnant. But darling, I wouldn't trade it. I got you. And California... well, it'll still be there when I'm ready. Maybe Devon will take me someday."

Dillon instantly regretted bringing it up. Wanting to lift the mood, he changed the subject.

"How about we swing by The Swamp and pick up my tips from last night? I'll buy you a burger."

Denise smiled, walking back to the truck. "Okay, honey, that sounds good. I could use a drink anyway."

Dillon drove them to The Swamp. The bar looked quiet as they pulled into the lot. The front door stood open, inviting customers in on the warm fall afternoon.

He parked near the entrance. The truck door slammed behind him as he stepped out. Glancing back, he saw his mother following close behind.

Julio sat at the end of the bar, his head down as he sifted through a stack of paperwork. The bartender moved between cleaning and restocking the shelves. He gave Dillon a nod of acknowledgment. Dillon nodded back and walked over to stand beside Julio.

Julio paused what he was doing and greeted him with a smile. "Hola, brother. What's happening?"

Dillon patted his friend on the shoulder. "Hey, man. I thought I'd grab my tips if you've got a minute."

Julio pushed his stool back and stood. "Sure, they're in the office. Let's go get them."

Denise slid onto an empty stool nearby and waved at the bartender. "What's a woman gotta do to get a drink around here?"

The bartender paused mid-unpacking, eyeing Denise carefully. He glanced over her shoulder at Dillon with a silent question. Dillon sighed and shrugged in response.

Julio ignored the exchange and headed toward the back of the building. Dillon followed.

The office was a small, windowless room cluttered with bare essentials. Open boxes of random bar supplies filled every available surface. Julio dropped into the chair and leaned forward to open the safe while Dillon stood in the doorway, surveying the mess.

Julio retrieved a bundle of envelopes secured with a thin rubber band. He flipped through them until he found one with Dillon's name scrawled on the front. Tossing the rest back into the safe, he handed the envelope to Dillon.

"Thanks," Dillon began, but stopped short when he saw Julio's expression.

Julio leaned back in the chair, locking eyes with him. His face had gone solemn. He rocked back slightly and let out a deep breath, one that seemed to drain the room of its air. Tension suddenly thickened between them. For a moment, neither spoke.

Julio rested his arm on the desk and looked away. He inhaled slowly, then turned back to Dillon.

"I..." he began. "Dillon, have you heard about Arthur?"

Dillon blinked, confused. "What?" was all he could manage.

Julio's eyes grew heavy with sadness. "Dillon... he OD'd. They found him yesterday."

Dillon stared at Julio, blinking. The words hit him like a punch to the chest. His first thought was, This isn't funny. Who would joke about something like that?

Julio dropped his gaze to the floor. "I know how much you liked him. I didn't want to be the one to tell you."

The words drifted past Dillon like a breeze through the open door, but were incomprehensible. He heard them, but they didn't make sense. His feet felt heavy, glued to the floor. A pressure built in his head as he asked, barely above a whisper, his eyes beginning to blur, "I don't understand. Is he at the hospital? Or... his house?"

Julio stood and met his eyes again. "He's gone, buddy. The police are investigating, but it's pretty clear."

His heart sank and settled at the bottom of a dark well in Dillon's soul. Arthur, his mentor, his friend, was gone. Just like that.

Have you ever seen a flipbook? The kind where you flick the pages and one image blurs into the next to show movement? That's how memories played in Dillon's mind as he revisited his time with Arthur. He remembered being ten years old, sitting on the worn couch while waiting for his mom. Arthur had placed Dillon's fingers on the strings of a guitar. The joy he'd felt when Arthur gave him one for his birthday. Days spent on front porches, park benches, and stages. Most of the time, Arthur played alongside him. Sometimes, Arthur just watched. But always, he encouraged and guided Dillon.

Dillon would never call Arthur a father figure. He wasn't just a friend, either. Arthur had inspired him to believe in something beyond his surroundings. He gave Dillon hope, hope Arthur himself never felt.

Dillon swallowed hard and tried to clear his head. "That can't be right," he muttered.

In his mind, he saw Arthur onstage, guitar in hand, grinning under the lights. Arthur can't be dead. We've got a gig this weekend. We have a gig every weekend... here at the bar.

Julio's hand rested gently on Dillon's shoulder. In a daze, Dillon turned and walked toward the front of the building. Behind him, Julio's voice echoed faintly: "If you need to talk or anything…"

Dillon lifted a hand in a halfhearted wave and kept walking. Arthur had given Dillon something he never had himself: hope. And now, it felt pointless. Dillon needed to get out of the bar, the place he shared most with Arthur, and with his dreams of escaping this small town and small life.

As he reached the end of the bar, he started to collect himself. The bartender had gone back to stocking shelves and wiping surfaces. Julio's papers still sat undisturbed, and a single empty rocks glass marked the spot where his mother had been sitting.

He glanced around. "Where did she go?" he asked.

The bartender looked up. "She left a few minutes ago. Kept glancing at the door. I don't know, maybe she had somewhere to be."

"Where?"

The man shrugged. "No idea. Don't worry about the tab, though. Just so you know, she knocked back three whiskeys. She was wound tighter than a six-year-old on a sugar rush."

Dillon offered a quiet thanks and made his way to his truck. Behind the wheel, he sat for a moment, staring blankly at the dashboard. Then he started the engine and backed out of the lot, the only rational explanation for her disappearance beginning to form in his mind.

He pulled into Shots Fired Drive-Thru Drinks and spotted his mother standing on the sidewalk near the entrance, locked in a heated argument with a man. Dillon recognized him as the guy who worked the drive-thru window.

He parked and stepped out of the truck calmly. The shouting was loud as hell; everyone in town could probably hear it. Denise, though a good six inches shorter than the man, stood toe-to-toe with him, completely undeterred by the size difference. She pointed at him angrily.

"Don't try to cheat me! I know how much a fifth costs. This is highway robbery!"

The employee's face flushed red with anger. "I already told you," he snapped. "Prices haven't changed. I don't know what you're talking about. Get out of here before I call the cops."

Denise bristled. "You know damn well you're lying. I know what it costs. You just don't want to sell to me for some reason."

The man straightened, arms stiff at his sides, fists clenched tight. He looked like he might launch into the sky like a Roman candle. Grinding his teeth, he growled, "I sure as hell don't want to sell to you now. You are crazy!"

Dillon stepped between them. "Whoa, let's all calm down. What's going on?"

Denise pressed her lips together and glared. The man blinked at Dillon as if he'd just appeared out of thin air. Still fuming, he barely moved, but his voice came out a notch calmer.

"You need to get her out of here. That's my final warning."

"Hey, man," Dillon said, raising both hands in a peaceful gesture. "No worries. I got her."

Denise, still facing the man, barked, "He took my money! I want my damn whiskey."

Dillon looked between the two of them. The man blinked as Denise's words sank in and said, "She was a dollar sixty-one short. The bottle's still on the counter beside her money."

Dillon pulled the crumpled envelope from his pocket. It held his tips. "If I pay you what she's short, will you let her have the bottle?" he asked.

The clerk let the resolution settle in his mind. His irritation visibly eased. He looked at Dillon and replied, "Yeah, come inside." Then, with a flash of returning anger, he added, "But she has to stay out here!"

Dillon followed him into the store and stood at the counter while the clerk walked around to the register. Dillon handed him two bills. The clerk rang a no-sale and popped open the drawer. He slid his hand across the counter to scoop up the money Denise had left. He counted the money into the drawer and put the change on the counter to complete the sale. Dillon picked up the money while the man studied him.

"You look familiar. Do I know you?" the clerk asked.

Grasping the neck of the whiskey bottle from the counter, Dillon replied, "Maybe I just have one of those faces."

The man still looked like he was trying to place him as Dillon walked out of the store. The weight of life in this dead-end town pressed down on him. He had to get out.

"Jesus, Mom," Dillon burst out. "Can't you keep it together for a little while?"

Denise flinched and clutched the unopened bottle to her chest. Her voice trembled. "He was trying to cheat me. I'm your mother. You should be sticking up for me."

Dillon started the engine and threw the truck into reverse. He backed onto the road and headed home, his head pounding with the drama and embarrassment from the liquor store scene.

"It's okay," he muttered after a beat. "He probably rang it up wrong or something."

Denise looked like she might cry. "I would've given him the rest of the money. I didn't have it right then. You know I get my check on the third. I'll pay you back, honey."

Dillon's heart sank. He kept his eyes on the road. "Don't worry about it," he mumbled.

They drove the rest of the way in silence. Denise stared out the window, lost in her own world, watching the fields and buildings slide past. Dillon kept his eyes forward, but his mind wandered, from Arthur, to Greg, to wanting to ask his mother not to drink, at least not today. But he knew that was a hopeless request, one that would only bring more deflection and bitterness.

When they pulled into the yard, Denise climbed out before he even shut off the engine. She hugged the bottle tightly as she hurried up the steps into the trailer. Dillon let out a weary sigh and followed her inside.

He entered through the front door. In the kitchen, Denise was pouring whiskey over a glass of ice. Devon sat in his usual spot in front of the television. Neither of them acknowledged Dillon as he walked past and into his room, where he lay down on his bed and stared at the ceiling.

His thoughts churned, Arthur, Greg, and the liquor store scene all swirling in his mind. Before long, Dillon drifted into a fitful sleep.

He woke to the early morning sun peeking through the curtains. Blinking up at the ceiling, he lay still for a moment. Then he heard shouting and the sharp bang of something slamming from elsewhere in the trailer. He swung his feet over the side of the bed and sat up. The arguing grew louder and clearer.

"You crazy bitch!" Devon shouted.

Still wearing the clothes from the day before, Dillon ran a hand through his hair and stood. Another loud bang echoed through the house.

Devon's voice, edged with fury, echoed from outside. "Let me in the damn house! I'm not playing!"

Dillon walked into the living room. Denise stood in the kitchen, leaning against the counter, crying. He stepped closer, closing the short distance between them. The smell of alcohol and sweat clung to her.

Concerned and shaken, he asked, "Mom, what's wrong?"

She turned to look at him, cheeks streaked, eyes red. "Oh, honey, it's okay. We just had a little argument. Go on back to bed."

Dillon blinked in disbelief at her dismissal. "Did he hurt you?"

His eyes scanned her for signs of abuse, but he saw none.

"Of course not, honey," Denise said, her voice trembling through a sob. "You know Devon's just a big old teddy bear. He's just..." She hesitated, searching for the right word. "Passionate."

The front door rattled violently as Devon pounded on it with his fists.

"This is my damn house, too! Open the door!"

Dillon turned and opened it.

Devon blinked in surprise. He stood barefoot on the small wooden porch, wearing nothing but an open robe and boxers. Dillon almost laughed. He looked like a cross between a homeless man and a toddler caught stealing a cookie.

Devon gritted his teeth. "What do you want? Get out of my way."

Dillon stepped back from the doorway, his mother close behind. Devon stormed into the house and planted himself in the middle of the living room.

Denise exploded, her voice shrill with fury. "Can you believe he was hiding blow from me?"

Devon's lips curled into a smirk he couldn't quite suppress. "Come on. Blow? Who even calls it that anymore?"

"I can't believe you! Greedy son of a," Denise shouted, slamming her fist against a cupboard door. The sound cracked through the trailer.

Devon avoided her eyes, still deflecting. "Flake, maybe. Or powder. But blow? You sound like an '80s drug dealer."

Denise's wild stare shot from Devon to Dillon. Her voice cracked as she spat, "And do you know where he hid it?"

"Look," Devon said, his tone defensive with a touch of fake hurt. "You know I'm good at sharing. I was saving it for a special occasion, like date night."

Denise's body went rigid with rage. She turned back to Dillon, her voice rising again. "In the freaking shower rod! Who hides drugs in a shower rod?"

Dillon glanced at Devon, who was doing his best to look serious. Devon shrugged. "Seemed like a good idea to me. You didn't find it for..." He trailed off, realizing too late he'd said too much.

Denise gritted her teeth. Her voice dropped to a hiss, like a cornered bobcat. "What? How long?"

"Hey, look. You don't want that stuff just lying around," Devon said, trying to justify himself.

"You have an ounce of weed on your TV tray," Denise snapped. "Right there in the middle of the living room."

Dillon watched the two argue, weariness settling deep in his bones. He sighed and offered, "Guys, please calm down. Devon, can you put up your weed for a little while?"

Devon raised his voice, clearly exasperated. "Why? It's mine. I paid for it. And I don't know why you're telling me anything. You're just a punk kid."

Denise's tone simmered with warning. "Don't talk to him like that."

Devon turned on her, indignant. "He's not going to tell me what to do. I am the man of the house."

"Man of the house?" Denise shot back, her voice rising again. "This is my house. I let you move in."

Devon stared at her with cold contempt. "Maybe I should move out."

"Maybe you should," Denise said quietly.

Devon glanced around the room, eyes darting for an exit. Then he muttered, "Maybe your freeloading son should move out."

Denise looked like she'd been slapped. Her face went pale as she said firmly, "He isn't going anywhere."

Dillon stared at the floor for a moment before murmuring, "Maybe I should."

Silence settled over the room as Dillon lowered his head and turned away. Denise didn't look directly at him. She trembled, shaken by what he'd said and ashamed she had nothing to say in return. He walked slowly to his room, shut the door behind him, and cut off the argument before it could start again. Lying on his bed, he stared at the ceiling until sleep finally pulled him under.

When Dillon woke, it was nearly lunchtime. His stomach growled, and he had to pee. He got out of bed and picked out some fresh clothes. Something felt off. He couldn't quite place it, but a strange sense of change lingered in the air. Shrugging it off, he made his way to the bathroom for a shower and some relief.

From behind the door of his mother's bedroom, Devon's loud snores rumbled through the hallway.

Once clean and dressed, Dillon returned to his room. He glanced around at the piles of clothes, the unmade bed, and the cheap furniture crammed into the small space. Without emotion, he packed a gym bag with a few shirts and pairs of jeans. Into a side pocket, he tossed some guitar picks and a capo.

He swept his hair back from his face, took one last look around, and zipped the bag shut. A quiet emptiness settled over him as he slung the strap over his shoulder and stepped out of the trailer.

Dillon drove the small red truck through the still streets of downtown. The summer heat had eased, but the humidity clung stubbornly to the air. He pulled into the nearly empty bus station lot and parked in one of the vacant spots.

Climbing out, he looked down at the keys in his hand. With the bag over his shoulder and the keys still loosely gripped, he walked toward a pay phone at the far end of the lot.

He dropped the bag at his feet and set the keys and a handful of spare change on top of the phone. Fishing his wallet from his back pocket, he pulled out a worn slip of paper, Greg's cell number, scribbled in pencil.

Slotting two quarters into the machine, Dillon cradled the receiver between his chin and shoulder and dialed.

The ringtone buzzed twice before Greg picked up.

"Hello?" came the familiar voice.

Dillon exhaled, his shoulders relaxing. "Hey, man. What's going on?"

He could almost hear Greg's grin through the line.

"BROTHER! I can't believe you called," Greg said, his voice bright with excitement. "You should be here, Nashville is popping."

Dillon hesitated, searching for the right words.

Greg picked up on the pause. "Is everything okay?"

Dillon had rehearsed what he wanted to say, but now the words slipped away. He cleared his throat.

"It's alright. I was thinking I might come visit. I..."

Greg didn't let him finish.

"Yes! Dad rented me an apartment near campus. If you don't mind crashing on the couch. When are you getting here?"

Dillon exhaled slowly. Glancing up at the high midday sun, he replied, "Probably tomorrow. Depends on how long the bus takes."

Greg's voice bubbled with excitement. "Call me from the station, I'll come get you!"

Dillon hung up without saying goodbye. Slinging his bag over his shoulder, he grabbed the truck keys and walked toward the ticket counter.

The man behind the glass looked like he'd been working there since the station opened. His uniform matched the building, faded, worn, and lifeless.

Scowling at Dillon, he asked, "Where are you headed?"

"Nashville. One, please."

"That'll be $103.98," the man replied.

Dillon placed the truck keys on the counter and pulled out his wallet. He counted the cash and laid it beside the keys. The clerk took the money, slid a ticket under the glass, and said, "Bus leaves in an hour. Wait over there by the vending machines."

Dillon turned to go, but the man's gravelly voice stopped him.

"You forgot your keys."

Dillon paused and slowly turned back. His chest tightened as he considered what to say next.

"I found them in the parking lot," he said. "Maybe you could hold on to them in case someone comes looking."

Without waiting for a response, Dillon turned and walked away.

He could feel the pull of a better life if he could only reach it.

Chapter Four

The bus pulled into the station parking lot in Nashville. Dillon gazed out the window at the traffic and towering buildings. He felt small in this city of giant shadows and endless motion. Why did everyone seem to be in such a hurry?

As the bus came to a stop and the door creaked open, passengers began to file out. Two employees were already unloading suitcases and bags from the undercarriage onto the pavement when Dillon stepped off. He took a deep breath. The heavy Tennessee humidity hugged him. The sounds and smells hit him all at once. Dillon stretched, trying to shake off the weight of the city.

"This isn't so bad," he thought. "And this isn't hot. It's more stuffy. Hot is a heat dome in August with no swimming hole in sight." He retrieved his guitar case and backpack from the pile, then stepped onto the sidewalk and took in his surroundings.

A man caught his eye. He sat on the curb at the end of the sidewalk, his clothes tattered and stained, his hair matted and wild. He didn't look Dillon's way, even as Dillon watched him quietly ask passersby for change.

Dillon dug into his pocket and pulled out a handful of coins. He glanced around the station and spotted a row of vending machines. He walked over, dropped the coins one by one, and punched in the corresponding numbers. As the snacks fell, he collected them and returned to the man. The smell of piss and sweat rose from him. Dillon ignored it and handed the food over without a word. The man smiled as he accepted the offering.

Dillon turned and crossed the parking lot toward a pay phone near the edge. He reached into his pocket again, only to realize the receiver was disconnected from the cord. So much for that. He looked both ways down the street and watched as cars rushed past. Then he spotted a sign a few blocks away: "Cumberland Creek Saloon. Country Western Music. Food Served Until 1 AM."

Dillon headed toward it.

Inside the saloon, the contrast from the bright afternoon outside made the room feel even darker. He paused by the door as his eyes adjusted. The smell of beer-soaked wooden floors and disinfectant stirred familiar memories of The Swamp. Slowly, the scene came into focus: a long bar ran along the left wall, while round wooden tables filled most of the room. A raised stage stood at the far end. Bottles of every kind of liquor lined the shelves behind the bar, glowing in the dim light.

There were only a few people inside, a couple nursing drinks at the bar, a few more scattered at tables. The low chatter, the clinking of glassware, and the sight of people huddled in their private conversations brought a strange sense of comfort to Dillon. Maybe this place isn't so different, he thought.

Behind the bar stood a man who could only be described as a bear. He had a thick black beard and dark eyes that gleamed in the low light. He was massive, not like a football player, but more like a mountain of rubble. When he spoke, his voice boomed across the room.

"Come on in," he called. "Grab a stool and a drink. Welcome to Cumberland Creek Saloon, where the only thing stronger than our drinks are tomorrow's regrets."

Dillon approached the bar and stopped in front of the man.

"I was wondering if I could use your phone," he said. "I need to call my ride."

The man sized him up for a long moment. He didn't smile, and Dillon suddenly felt he'd made a mistake coming in. He was about to turn and leave when the man spoke again.

"You just got to town?"

Dillon stopped and turned back.

"Yeah," he answered, his voice more timid than he intended.

"You're a musician," the man said, not as a question, but a statement. "Here to make it big in Nashville."

Dillon flushed and shifted his guitar case in his hand.

"No, I mean, maybe. I don't know. I just got here."

The man studied him a moment longer, then added,

"You've got a guitar, and I'm guessing no money, since you're asking to use the phone."

Embarrassed, Dillon replied,

"Look, I just need to use a phone. I can pay you for it. You don't have to be an ass about it."

He thought he saw a glint in the man's eye, amusement, maybe.

"I'm Tim," the man said. "Owner of the place. Most folks call me Flumpy. Play me a song. If I like it, I'll let you borrow that phone."

"What?" was all Dillon could manage.

"I think that was a pretty simple request," Flumpy said, crossing his tree-sized arms over his massive chest. "Take your guitar over to the stage and play a song. Then I'll let you use the phone."

Dillon let out a small laugh and shook his head in disbelief. "Man, that's about as crazy as a cat herding cattle, but okay."

Flumpy watched as Dillon made his way to the stage and removed his guitar from its case. Dillon fumbled with the mic and flipped on the power. He strummed the guitar to check the tuning. Once everything was in place, he spoke into the microphone.

"Ladies and gentlemen," he began, "I'm Dillon Chillari. I've got a little song to share with you that a good man taught me some time back. This one's for you, Arthur."

Dillon held two fingers in the air, above his head, and looked up as he dedicated the song.

As Dillon played, the bar patrons paused what they were doing and turned to listen. Flumpy stood behind the bar, watching with rapt attention. The music, gentle and melodic, filled the room. When he finished, Dillon thanked the crowd and returned to speak with Flumpy.

Flumpy remained in the same spot where Dillon had left him, showing no clear sign of whether he liked the song or not. Between them on the bar sat a plate of fries and a burger.

"Sit down and eat," Flumpy instructed. "I'll get you something to drink."

Dillon sat, his expression confused. "I just need a phone."

"Oh yeah," Flumpy said, as if the thought had just occurred to him. He placed a silver Razor phone on the bar beside the plate. "You can eat while you wait for your ride." He pulled a soda from the gun and set it next to the meal.

"I can pay," Dillon insisted as he sat. His stomach growled, a reminder he hadn't eaten since leaving Louisiana.

Flumpy huffed and walked down the bar to serve another customer.

Dillon flipped open the phone and called Greg. He finished the burger and sipped on the soda as he watched the comings and goings around him. Most of the patrons called Flumpy by name. The rush was outside, not here. It felt like the world beyond the front door was far away, and Dillon was just fine being right here.

Greg walked into the bar and spotted Dillon. He took the stool beside him. Behind the counter, an auburn-haired girl was unloading glasses from a box. Her hair fell around her bare shoulders. Both boys noticed her firm thighs under the cutoff jean shorts and her no-nonsense attitude as she worked.

Flumpy stepped between the girl and the boys' view. He addressed Greg. "What can I get you?"

Greg looked at the taps. "What craft beers do you have?"

Without answering, Flumpy poured a draft and set it in front of him. "We have PBR. I'll open you a tab. Enjoy." Without another word, he walked away, leaving the boys to talk.

Greg turned to Dillon with a grin. "Welcome to Nashville. I've missed you, brother. What's up with the big guy?"

Dillon leaned in for a quick hug. "That's Flumpy, the owner. Interesting guy, for sure."

Greg laughed. "Flumpy? What kind of name is that?"

Still stacking glasses, the girl chimed in without looking up. "He hooked up with some drunk girl one night. She tried to say he was 'fucking lumpy,' but it came out 'Flumpy.' The name stuck."

The guys burst out laughing.

Greg raised an eyebrow and said, "That's a good story. More importantly, what's your name?"

"Aubrey," she replied. "Stick around, and I might tell you about his best friend, Johnny Rawdog." She gave Dillon a sly look as she spoke.

Dillon tried to stay casual. "What's your story?"

Aubrey narrowed her eyes, sizing him up. "My story? What do you want to know?"

Dillon felt out of his depth. He wasn't a ladies' man. One of the few things that could genuinely make his mother mad was being rude to a woman. She wasn't here, but the weight of not disappointing her was. Dillon coughed and asked, "Are you from here?"

Aubrey stopped stacking glasses and walked over to the bar. The wooden counter that separated them seemed to shrink as she came closer.

"You're going to have to do better than that," she teased. "Name, rank, and serial number are questions for first dates and interrogations." She watched him squirm with a playful gleam in her eye. Then she added, "We're all from somewhere else. In five years of working at this bar, I've met one guy from Nashville. He was the mayor's son."

Dillon's curiosity sparked, and he didn't want to lose her attention. But Greg drained his beer and stood. That's just how Greg was. If he wasn't doing what he wanted, he got up and left. He could be oblivious to anything he wasn't directly involved in.

He dropped some cash on the bar. "Let's get out of here," he said to Dillon. Then, to Aubrey: "Thanks for the beer."

Dillon stood, then glanced across the bar at Flumpy. "Thanks for the food. Do I pay you?" he called out, raising a hand to catch his attention.

Flumpy crossed the room in giant strides, his expression unreadable.

"No worries, my friend. Lunch is on me. I need a new guitar player for the house band. The last one didn't come back after a disagreement with the lead singer. If you can play like you did a minute ago and show up on time, I'll give you a shot. Come in tomorrow, we'll work out the details."

Dillon smiled. "We'll see. I appreciate it." He turned to Aubrey with a grin. "I'll be back."

She smiled playfully. "Of course you will."

Dillon took another look around the bar. The faint smell of stale beer and the worn wooden floor held stories. Arthur would've liked this place, he thought.

"Dude," Greg said, shaking his head, "you've been here, like, thirty seconds, and you already have a job. What's up with that?"

Dillon laughed and followed his friend out of the bar.

They drove to Greg's apartment in his Impala.

"It's not far," Greg explained. "Everything downtown is laid out on this grid. Heck, given the traffic, it's faster to walk most places. Living in the West End is definitely da bomb."

Inside, Dillon noted that the apartment was clean, orderly, and decorated much like Greg's parents' house. Greg stood in the center of the living room and gestured as he spoke.

"My bedroom's back there. That's the bathroom, kitchen, and balcony. The couch, your bed."

Dillon sat on the sofa, looking around. "Thanks for letting me crash here for a while," he said. "Back home... it was just too much."

"No problem," Greg replied cheerfully. "You don't need to explain. Stay as long as you want. Oh, and I'm having a party tonight. Just a couple guys from school."

"Party?" Dillon perked up. "I'm in."

Greg laughed. "It'll be a small one."

Dillon leaned back on the couch and propped his feet up. This is going to be alright, he thought. He hadn't realized how exhausted he was. Within minutes, he drifted off to sleep.

A few hours later, Dillon woke. Greg had left him alone in the apartment. Dillon rose from the couch and explored the space. The refrigerator held a few beers, a half-eaten pizza, and a partial bottle of orange juice. Dillon shrugged. He guessed college life meant no more of Momma's home cooking. Too bad. He liked that jambalaya she made.

Dillon turned on the shower, picked up a towel from the floor, and shook it out before laying it across the toilet lid. He pulled his shirt over his head as steam began to rise from the running water. Once under the hot stream, he thought about all the miles he had traveled and the new world that lay ahead. He watched the water swirl down the drain, carrying every day before this one with it.

After his shower, Dillon wrapped a towel around his waist, brushed back his long hair with one hand, and walked into the living room to grab clothes from his backpack. He shook out a clean pair of jeans just as the apartment door opened. Greg walked in, followed by several guys and girls, all laughing and joking. Greg carried a twelve-pack of beer under one arm, while the others set bottles of liquor on the kitchen counter. Everyone seemed familiar with the place. One guy pulled plastic cups from a cabinet and started pouring drinks.

Greg set the beer on the coffee table and laughed. "Hey man, it's not that kind of party. Put some clothes on."

Dillon flushed and smiled back at his friend. He grabbed a T-shirt from his bag and took his clothes into the bathroom to change.

Once dressed, Dillon returned to the living room. In his brief absence, the number of people had grown. Music played, and no one paid him much attention as he moved through the crowd toward Greg. When he reached him, Greg slung an arm around Dillon's shoulder and flashed his biggest Cheshire cat smile.

"Hey, everybody! This is Dillon, my best friend from back home. Make him feel welcome."

A few people cheered, and some of the guys near Dillon greeted him warmly. One handed him a red plastic cup half-filled with something strong. The scent of tequila hit Dillon as he took a sip.

"Thanks," he said toward the general direction the cup had come from.

Dillon felt a bit out of place. The other guests were college students, affluent, confident. They dressed and carried themselves like Greg. They were his people in a way Dillon wasn't, and never would be. The thought sat heavy in Dillon's chest. Greg was his best friend. Back home, people with little to show mingled with people who had a lot. This wasn't that. Dillon hoped he could find a place in the new life Greg had built. He drank deeply from the sweet, burning liquid and wandered through the crowd.

Dillon had no idea how long the party lasted. People seemed to come and go in waves, but the apartment was always full. At one point, while standing beside Greg on the balcony, Dillon asked, "Why hasn't anyone called the cops? There are a lot of people in here."

Greg laughed. "A bunch of these people are neighbors. This building mostly rents to kids from the campus. You don't have to worry about the cops."

Then Greg turned serious. "You having a good time?"

"Yeah, for sure," Dillon replied absently. The truth was, he wondered if he fit in with this group. He wasn't the big, loud, funny guy like Greg, someone everyone wanted to be friends with. He wasn't surprised Greg had built a whole new life in this city. You could strand Greg on a desert island, and he'd make friends with the fish and have the birds delivering pizza inside a week.

Dillon felt most comfortable on stage, where an invisible line separated him from the crowd.

"I need another drink." He turned and made his way through the crowd to the kitchen.

He refilled his cup from the growing collection of mixers and liquor bottles on the kitchen counter. As he turned toward the small table between the kitchen and the living room, he noticed four guys gathered around it. In the center were five shot glasses, one placed right in the middle.

One of the guys looked up. Dillon asked, "What are y'all playing?"

"Chandelier. Ever heard of it?"

At that moment, another guy bounced a quarter on the table. It landed in the glass nearest the first speaker, who downed the shot in one gulp.

"No," Dillon said with a shrug. "That's a new one on me."

The guy wiped his mouth and refilled his glass. "It's Quarters, but everyone has their glass. If the quarter lands in yours, you drink. If it lands in the center glass, everyone drinks, and the last one to finish has to take the center shot too."

"Okay, I'll give it a try," Dillon said, nodding as he took a seat.

The quarter was passed to him. It clinked loudly as he bounced it on the table, then landed with a splash in the center glass. The guys grabbed their glasses and drank. Dillon raced to keep up. The center glass slid toward him as laughter bubbled around the table.

Dillon did his best to keep pace. The liquor did its job, and Dillon started to feel the effects. He found it easier to talk to the guys at the table. He watched the flow of people through the apartment and clung to the edge he'd found.

What would it be like to have the money and freedom, the future, all these people around him had? He found a seat on the end of the sofa and drunkenly wondered, What would they say to me if I became a big star?

He leaned back and thought proudly, A big star, that's what I need to be. Play music all day, and none of you would look down on me.

Dillon woke up on the couch, slumped at one end where he'd passed out. A dull ache throbbed behind his eyes, a hangover from the night before. He blinked to clear his vision and scanned the room, taking in the mess left behind by the guests.

Greg strolled into the living room from his bedroom, looking fresh and ready to take on the day, as usual. He smiled and asked cheerfully, "So, what do you think? Did you have a good time?"

"I think so," Dillon replied, stretching as he tried to shake the cobwebs from his head. "This place is trashed."

"No worries," Greg said with a shrug. "The maid comes tomorrow. We just need to pick up the beer cans and the big stuff."

"The maid?" Dillon echoed, raising an eyebrow.

"Yeah," Greg said offhandedly. "My parents dropped by unexpectedly a while back and weren't too impressed with my housekeeping skills. So now my mom pays for a maid to come by a couple of times a week. She'll be here tomorrow."

"It's not a big deal," Greg added flatly. "Anyway, are you going to talk to that bar owner about playing at his place?"

Dillon sat up and looked at his friend. He thought about sitting on the stage yesterday, the guitar in his hands as he sang into the mic. "I can. But that might mean crashing on your couch for a while. I don't know how long."

Greg met his gaze with quiet understanding. "I already told you, I don't care how long you stay. Do what you need to do. I've got your back."

Dillon gave a small nod, his gratitude unspoken but clear.

CHAPTER FIVE

Dillon walked into the bar. Flumpy was behind it, just as he had been the day before when Dillon stopped by. Dillon approached and paused in front of him. Flumpy looked down at him, his expression unchanged.

Breaking the silence, Dillon said, "Hey. I came back to talk to you about that job, playing with the band."

Flumpy appraised Dillon quietly. Seconds passed slowly before he finally spoke. "You did pretty well when you played your solo. Tell me, what brought you here?"

Dillon gathered his thoughts and began, "I've been playing since I was a kid. Mostly blues, classic rock, some zydeco. I've been with a bar band back home since I was sixteen, that's the youngest they'll let you work in a bar there."

Flumpy stared at him, thinking. "You think you can play cold? Just jump in without practicing with the guys?"

Dillon felt a stab of frustration. He'd expected to walk in and get the job. What was with all the questions?

"I think so," he said, then coughed. He took a deep breath and looked Flumpy in the eye. "Yes. I can play cold. You just have to let me show you."

Flumpy looked away, rubbing a bar towel back and forth on the service line behind him.

"The band plays for tips. I need you here by seven, Wednesday through Saturday, ready to go. If you're late or can't deliver, there are no second chances."

Dillon hesitated. "Tips? I thought this was a paid gig. And how am I supposed to know what's on the set list?"

Flumpy turned and picked up a piece of paper from the counter behind him.

"Here's the set list," he said, handing it to Dillon. "I'm guessing you can get the sheet music if you need it."

Dillon took the paper automatically and scanned the list. Relief washed over him; he already knew several of the songs. He figured he could find a library and use a public computer to download the rest.

Flumpy spoke again. "Think of it like commission: the more people you entertain, the more that show up, and the more tips you make. I don't skim anything for the house. Plus, my vocalist's been pulling in a solid crowd ever since I took over this place."

"Okay, I guess," was all he managed to say.

Flumpy nodded, his tone flat. "I'll see you on Wednesday. Seven o'clock."

Dillon turned toward the door, dazed, and began walking. As he passed the end of the bar, Aubrey called out to him.

"Hey, you. Come here."

Dillon walked over and stood with the bar between them. He looked at her blankly, then blurted, "You have the greenest eyes."

Aubrey laughed in a light, airy sound that captured Dillon's imagination. It made him think of warm afternoons in the bayou.

"Lean over here," she said, her voice soft but firm.

Dillon leaned across the bar. Aubrey reached out, her fingers brushing his face, tracing the stubble that had begun to grow along his jawline.

"I like a man with a beard," she said, eyeing the thin line of hair. "It's manly."

Dillon stared into her eyes, transfixed. Then she withdrew her hand and stepped back from the bar.

Snapping out of the trance, Dillon smirked.

"I still don't know where you're from."

"See you on Wednesday," she said with a coy smile.

Dillon left the bar in a daze. It had all happened so quickly. He imagined Aubrey's smile and laugh, replaying the conversation with Flumpy in his head. "Tips? "he thought. "I'll give it a try. I can always quit. Surely, it's not hard to find a gig in the home of country music." Dillon touched his wallet in his jeans. "It better work. I'm going to be broke soon if it doesn't."

Dillon quickly discovered that Greg had fully embraced the college lifestyle. Parties were a regular occurrence at the apartment. While Dillon liked Greg's college friends, he often found himself staying up late, unable to sleep with the couch situated in the middle of the apartment's busiest social hub. Grateful for Greg's hospitality, he chose not to complain. Instead, he spent as much time as possible outside, exploring the city on foot.

Nashville buzzed with life. Everywhere Dillon turned, he encountered history and music. It felt as though the city's heartbeat pulsed to the rhythm of a country song, and Dillon loved it. He often stopped to watch street performers or lingered outside music venues, soaking in the sound of incredibly talented artists. Horse-drawn carriages strolled down the streets carrying couples, and bachelorette parties were everywhere. He was amazed by how many women were out celebrating their upcoming weddings.

One sight especially amused him: a contraption called a "pedal pub." It was a four-wheeled bicycle with bench seats for about a dozen people, arranged around a central bar. A bartender stood in the middle, serving drinks while the group pedaled together to move the vehicle. It always looked like a blast.

Wednesday came quickly. Dillon felt nervous. He wasn't sure what to expect, but he was confident in his music. Guitar in hand, he walked into the bar. Aubrey and Flumpy were busy behind the counter, serving drinks. Aubrey smiled when their eyes met.

Just then, a busboy carrying a tub of dirty dishes bumped into him. He paused and said, "Hey, the new guy! The band's tuning up on stage. I'm Johnny, by the way." Johnny had long, dishwater-blond hair tied back in a ponytail and a matching beard, also tied. He looked more like a roadie than a bar-back, but Dillon wasn't one to judge. He nodded and weaved through the small crowd toward the stage. The bar wasn't packed, but he didn't let that discourage him.

He stepped onto the stage and observed the band members making last-minute adjustments, tuning instruments, shifting cords, and fiddling with amp knobs. One of them turned to Dillon and extended a hand. "I'm

Tyler. That's Blake. And Bill plays drums." Bill saluted Dillon with one of his drumsticks. Blake smiled in his direction as he continued tuning his bass.

"Good to meet y'all," Dillon said, feeling a little out of place.

"Have you played around here before?" Tyler asked.

Dillon flushed as he explained, "I'm brand new to the city, though I was in a band back in Louisiana. It was the weirdest thing, Flumpy just told me to show up and play."

Tyler had a boyish grin for a man in his forties. He smiled hospitably at Dillon. "You'll get used to him. He's a good guy, and he's got the biggest heart. I once saw him stop traffic in front of the bar to rescue a cat that was stuck in the middle."

"That's a nice thing to do," Dillon commented.

"Yeah," Tyler replied, "that cat clawed him up pretty good. He looked like he got slapped with a rake."

Dillon didn't know if he should smile, so he turned his attention to his guitar. Tyler leaned over and pointed to a guy at the bar. He was tall, broad-shouldered, and stood out from the crowd. Sandy blond hair peeked from beneath a black cowboy hat. He wore a black silk shirt with pearl buttons, crisp blue jeans, and boots. When he smiled at a nearby woman, his perfect teeth flashed in the light. He downed a shot, turned to the stage, and in three confident strides, was standing at the microphone.

Tyler said under his breath, "Here comes another questionable decision."

Wasting no time, the man leaned into the mic and said, "Good evening, everybody. I'm Boone Kane, and I'm here to party." He half-turned and noticed Dillon. Placing his hand over the microphone, he said to him, "Oh, a new guy. Let's see if you last the night. We've got enough dead weight around here." Then he dropped his hand and spoke into the mic again. "Count us in, Bill."

The drummer called out, "One, two, three!"

Dillon stood still as the rest of the band launched into the first song on the set list. Boone began to sing. He shot Dillon a sharp glance. That snapped Dillon out of his trance, and he began to play.

Boone sang and played to the crowd all evening. He eagerly accepted shots from audience members and flirted shamelessly with the women. At one point, he pointed to a beautiful woman standing beside her boyfriend near the stage.

"Aren't you just the prettiest filly in the field tonight? Why don't you come up on stage with me?"

The woman blushed. Her boyfriend hesitated, then gave her an encouraging nudge. Boone extended his hand, and she stepped up to stand beside him. The crowd erupted in cheers. Boone launched into a slow song. As he sang, he slipped an arm around her waist and pulled her closer. He gazed into her eyes, swaying with the music. She blushed again, unsure of what to do. Hoots and hollers rose from the audience. Boone's hand slid down to rest on her ass.

Her boyfriend shouted, "Hey! That's enough!" and moved closer to the stage.

Boone ignored him, continuing to serenade the woman. She smiled, caught up in the attention and the energy of the moment. Her boyfriend reached out, but a bouncer placed a firm hand on his shoulder. He let his hand fall, surrendering, his face tight with concern.

As the song ended, the woman glanced around the room, her expression heated and dreamy. Her boyfriend took her hand and helped her off the stage. Boone leaned into the mic.

"Honey, you should stick around till after the show."

The boyfriend's face flushed with anger. He glared at Boone but caught sight of the bouncer looming behind him. Leaning in, he whispered something to the woman, then gently pulled her along as they headed for the door. She cast a furtive smile at Boone and followed her boyfriend out.

Boone winked at her retreating figure, then turned back to the crowd.

"Y'all, we're gonna take a break now. Don't go anywhere, we'll be back in fifteen minutes."

He covered the mic with his hand and turned toward the band.

"You need to get your act together. You sound like crap."

Boone hopped off the stage and made his way to the bar, laughing with nearby patrons and raising his shot glass in a toast.

Dillon removed his guitar strap and set the instrument on an empty stand. He turned to Blake nearby.

"What's his problem?" Dillon asked.

Blake removed his guitar and replied, "He's a jerk. Just ignore him."

He gave Dillon a quick once-over and added, "We're going out back for a smoke if you wanna come."

Dillon followed the band members through a large metal door behind the stage.

Outside, they stood in a narrow alley paved with uneven cobblestones. There was no sidewalk, just a blue dumpster and a lone streetlight casting dim light from the corner.

Tyler spoke first. "You did alright."

"What's the story with Boone?" Dillon asked.

Blake laughed. "He's a jerk. Won some local singing contest on TV, and now he thinks he's gonna be the next big country star."

Blake flicked his cigarette butt to the ground and stomped it out.

"Truth is," he said, "Boone's the least likely to make it. He's a drunk and a womanizer. Hell, he doesn't even perform anywhere else but here. The rest of us are studio musicians."

"Does he act like that all the time?" Dillon asked.

Billy tossed his cigarette to the street and gave Dillon a reassuring pat on the shoulder.

"Don't worry about him, boy. He's a little fish in a big, big pond. He's only here because Flumpy feels indebted to him. Boone brought a good crowd when the bar first opened. I suspect even Flumpy has his limits."

The band headed back to the stage to prepare for the next set. Boone was still at the end of the bar, entertaining a crowd. He downed a tall glass of something dark and fizzy in one gulp. Dillon guessed it was whiskey and soda. Boone laughed and slapped the counter.

Flumpy had materialized behind the mic, holding a bright yellow plastic bucket high above his head. He watched warily as Boone made his way back to the stage.

Flumpy raised his voice almost to a shout. "Most of y'all know that what we make at the door goes to pay the band," he said. "Thanks for coming out and supporting live music in the greatest city ever known for country music."

The crowd responded with whoops and cheers. Flumpy waited for quiet, then continued.

"If you liked what you heard tonight, drop a tip in the bucket for the band. I know they'll appreciate it."

From somewhere in the crowd, a drunken voice cried out, "Praise the Lord and pass the bucket!"

Flumpy chuckled and handed the bucket to someone near the stage. The man dropped in a dollar and passed it along. The bucket disappeared into the crowd, reappearing every so often before eventually making its way back to Aubrey at the bar, who kept an eye on it.

Flumpy stepped offstage, and Boone took his place at the mic.

"Okay, Nashville! It's time to party!" he shouted, pointing back at Billy.

Billy began to play, and the rest of the band joined in.

Boone kept up the act as the band's flamboyant front man. By the end of the night, he was drunk, even stumbling into Billy's drum kit near the end of the set. After the final song, Boone left the stage and made a beeline for the bar.

"Give me one more for the road," he demanded.

"You're drunk and cut off," Aubrey shot back.

"That's bull," he slurred. "I need a drink, and then I'm taking this young lady home with me." He slapped the butt of a cute girl standing beside him. She smiled coyly but said nothing.

"I don't think you heard me," Aubrey said, raising her voice.

Flumpy caught her eye from the other end of the bar. He frowned, held up one finger, and mouthed, "Make it a weak one."

"Okay," Aubrey relented. She filled a glass with cola and made an exaggerated pour from a whiskey bottle. Her finger covered the spout, letting just enough liquor slip in to pool at the top. She slid it across the bar and asked, "How are you planning to pay for that?"

Boone wrapped an arm around the girl and replied, "Put it on my tab."

Aubrey's frustration was obvious. "You don't have a tab."

Boone grabbed the drink and turned his back to her. "I'll take it up with senior management."

Leaning on the girl for support, Boone whispered something and laughed with her. They made their way toward the exit, Boone sipping as they walked. He set the empty glass on the end of the bar by the door and left without another word.

Dillon had watched the whole scene unfold as he unplugged his guitar and packed it into its case. He walked down to the bar and asked Aubrey, "Is he always like that?"

Aubrey scowled. "No. Sometimes he's worse."

"Why does Flumpy put up with him?" Dillon asked.

Aubrey shrugged. "I guess he's cheap, and it's hard to find someone who shows up. They've got history."

Dillon glanced toward the front door Boone had exited through. When he turned back, Aubrey was pulling bills from the yellow tip bucket and sorting them into piles on the bar. Once she finished, she waved a hand toward the remaining band members still lingering near the stage.

"Hey, boys!" she called.

They each came down to the bar, and Aubrey handed out stacks of crumpled bills. They muttered thank you, stuffed the money into their pockets, and made their way toward the door. Bill gave Dillon a friendly slap on the shoulder. "You did well tonight. Hope you come back and play with us again."

"I'll see you tomorrow night," Dillon replied, smiling.

Bill smiled warmly in return and left with the others.

The bar had mostly emptied. Closing time was near. Patrons, in various stages of inebriation, made plans for late-night breakfasts or rides home. Aubrey leaned against the bar, a crumpled stack of bills in one hand. She smirked at Dillon, her tone flirtatious.

"Here are your tips, cowboy. Think you'll be back tomorrow?"

Dillon leaned in, their faces just inches apart. "Why does everyone keep asking if I'll be back? I thought this was an ongoing gig."

"It is," Aubrey said, waving the bills teasingly. "But it's a bit much for some people, especially Boone..." Her voice trailed off. Then she added, "I've been here a long time. A lot drink their tips away or can't cut the late nights. It's not for everybody."

Dillon took the money from her hand, straightened up, and began counting it. "Maybe some people don't need the money," he said.

He stuffed the cash into his front pocket. Aubrey returned to cleaning behind the bar.

She paused for a moment and said to Dillon, "Vicksburg."

Dillon looked at her, puzzled.

"Vicksburg, Mississippi," she clarified. "If you can't remember the questions, I'll stop giving you the answers. Bartending here seemed like a better choice than working in the casinos."

She resumed cleaning.

Dillon nodded, remembering he'd asked if she was from Nashville. A flicker of confidence stirred in his chest. She had been thinking about him. He was sure of it.

His gaze shifted to Flumpy, who stood by the front door. Flumpy's voice cut through the quieting room.

"Okay, folks, it's time to go. You don't have to go home, but you can't stay here!"

As Dillon passed him on the way out, he felt the need to say something. Flumpy looked at him with an unreadable expression.

"See you tomorrow," Dillon offered.

Flumpy nodded and turned back to usher out the last of the lingering patrons.

Dillon arrived at the apartment to find the party in full swing.

This is going to get old, he thought. Morning was only a few hours away, and he was exhausted.

He pushed through a crowd of drunken college students, stashed his guitar in a closet, and turned around just in time to see Greg chatting with two girls a few feet away.

He walked over. Greg spotted him and grinned.

"Hey, brother! I'm glad you're home. Meet the Brendas."

The two blonde girls looked so alike they could've been sisters, slim, bubbly, and practically bouncing in sync as they chatted excitedly.

"I'm Brenda Gayle, and this is Brenda Jean," one of them said.

"We're, like, the best friends ever," the other added.

"BFFs," Brenda Gayle chimed in.

"Yeah," Brenda Jean nodded. "We do everything together."

"Everything," Brenda Gayle echoed, biting her lip as she stared at Dillon.

"Uh, okay," Dillon replied awkwardly.

"Mind if I crash in your room?" he asked Greg.

"You know I don't mind, buddy," Greg said distractedly. "But I think someone's already in there. Grab a beer and enjoy the party."

"For sure," Dillon said, heading to the kitchen. He opened the fridge and pulled out a can of beer.

He yawned as he cracked it open and scanned the room.

The same group of guys was still playing Chandelier at the kitchen table. Dillon nodded at them, and they greeted him back. He weaved through the crowd, exchanging polite smiles and nods as people called out to him.

When he reached Greg's bedroom door, he peeked inside. Sure enough, a guy was sprawled face-down on the bed, fully clothed and lying spread-eagle, snoring loudly. Dillon thought about how much Greg had changed since high school. Back then, Greg would never have let someone crash in his bed or leave a mess. Now, the apartment was a disaster zone more often than not. Still, Dillon felt grateful that Greg was always there for him. One day, he'd repay him, big time.

Not quite sure what to do next, Dillon returned to the living room and sat on the edge of the couch, beer in hand. He took a sip and watched the party swirl around him. He thought about his interaction with Aubrey tonight. Thinking of her made him feel warm inside in a way he hadn't in a long time. Boone, on the other hand, was a nightmare. The band, though, was solid. He could learn a lot from them. He'd stick around for a while. There was more good than bad for him at the Cumberland Creek Saloon.

Chapter Six

Nights playing in the band were comfortable for Dillon. Boone, on the other hand, was always like watching a slow-motion car wreck. He drank like the bar had a whiskey spigot labeled just for him and often picked up women straight from the stage. Sometimes, he slurred his lyrics or barked angry orders at the rest of the band, who usually ignored him. Boone had peaked, and the only person who didn't seem to realize it was Boone himself.

Tonight looked to be no different. Dillon stood on stage, surveying the bar's patrons. His mind drifted to the past year, sleeping on Greg's couch, working at the bar. Greg never asked when he was getting his place or when he'd start paying rent, but Dillon still felt like it was time for a change. He stroked his now full beard. The bar was maybe a quarter full, possibly a bit more. Boone was late, as usual. Flumpy seemed to tolerate a lot from Boone, and Dillon often wondered if he'd ever reach his limit. Boone wasn't exactly packing the place. Most West End bars with live music pulled in bigger crowds.

Suddenly, the front door swung open and slammed into the nearby railing.

"WOOOO!" Boone bellowed, making a grand entrance. "The undiscovered king of country is here!"

There was a gleam in his eye. Dillon recognized it. For all Boone's flaws, he had that undeniable aura of stardom. Dillon felt a tug in his chest. He understood that need, to be adored, to captivate an audience, to be the person everyone watched. Boone may have missed his shot anywhere else, but in here... Boone had made it.

Dillon watched Boone cause his usual disruption. His eyes flicked to Flumpy, who was watching Boone closely but stayed put. Dillon turned back just in time to see

Boone stumble and catch himself on the bar. Boone straightened, then slurred,

"It's okay. I don't go down that easily."

His eyes landed on a girl nearby. "I wonder if we can say the same about you."

A man, presumably her boyfriend, stood up from the table beside her. His voice was sharp with anger.

"I realize you're drunk, but you better watch your mouth around her."

Boone chuckled and sneered. "You're lucky I've got someplace to be."

He staggered toward the stage. Dillon watched as Flumpy made a quick hand signal, prompting Johnny to quietly move behind Boone. Flumpy's face was clouded with worry. Boone lifted one booted foot onto the stage and gestured toward Aubrey.

"Make me a drink. I'll be right back to get it."

Aubrey ignored the command and continued serving a customer.

People sitting and standing nearby began to take notice. As Boone tried to complete his step onto the stage, his body suddenly shifted backward, almost in slow motion. His arms flew skyward. The foot he'd planted on the stage shot forward, while his trailing foot slammed into the riser with a loud thud. He slipped and fell. The crowd instinctively parted to make room for his crash.

A loud "OOF!" escaped as his back hit the floor. Johnny immediately stepped in and knelt at Boone's side.

"You okay?" he asked, trying to hide a grin. He squatted, forearms resting on his thighs, watching Boone struggle to get his bearings.

Boone lay stunned, red-faced, breathless, eyes darting to the faces around him. A couple of people covered their mouths in shock; more than a few laughed openly. Johnny slid one hand under Boone's shoulder and the other beneath his arm to help him up.

Humiliated, Boone sat up. "Let go of me!" he barked.

He rolled onto all fours, hanging his head in silence for a few moments. Then, slowly, he got to his knees, then to his feet. He stood unsteadily, eyes locking on Flumpy across the bar. Flumpy nodded toward the door.

Everyone who worked there had wondered what would finally be Flumpy's breaking point. A flicker of regret crossed the bar owner's face.

Johnny placed a hand on Boone's back and gently urged him toward the front of the bar. Boone hesitated, locking eyes with Flumpy.

"You can't," Boone began.

Flumpy simply said, "Enough is enough."

He had stayed loyal to Boone for as long as he could. In the early days of the bar, Flumpy had given a younger Boone his first shot on the stage. They were the new kids on the block, together. Boone had entered a televised contest that showcased local talent and quickly became the show's darling. His playful flirting with the crowd and bold stage presence made it clear he was going places.

But most of all, Boone could sing.

He captured the tone and depth of every song, drawing fans into the dreams he painted with each lyric.

In the end, though, Boone didn't win.

He didn't get the record deal. He didn't get the big prize check. He didn't land the bigger venues.

He didn't get his dream.

Flumpy knew all of this. He appreciated the larger crowds Boone's brief fame brought. He stuck by Boone when the crowds thinned, when the drinks came too easily, and when Boone seemed to be clinging to fame with both hands.

It hurt to make the call, but Flumpy had a business to run.

He couldn't keep risking everything to repay the same old debt to Boone, not for the thousandth time.

Without another word, Boone let Johnny lead him out of the bar.

Boone knew it, too.

Dillon turned to Tyler. "What do we do now?"

Tyler shrugged. Blake grabbed a rag and started wiping down the guitar slung across his neck. Billy sat behind the drums, watching like he was enjoying a wrestling match at the VFW.

Dillon turned back to Flumpy, who was now staring at him.

Dillon lifted his shoulders in a helpless shrug.

Flumpy mouthed, slow and clear: "Play."

Dillon had stood behind the mic more times than he could count, but this time felt different.

A knot twisted in his stomach. Bile rose in the back of his throat.

The room was dead silent, and all eyes seemed to be on him.

He gathered his thoughts. Arthur, his mentor, would've told him to pull it together. He could almost hear Arthur's voice: They're here to watch you play, not stand around. Give them what they came for.

Dillon looked back at the rest of the band.

"Do you know YOLO by Cotton Clifton?" he asked.

The guys nodded, visibly relaxing. Dillon felt some of the weight melt from his shoulders. It was his turn in the spotlight, and he was going to do it right. He wouldn't freeze, not like Boone. Would he?

He stepped up to the mic and said, "I know y'all came out tonight for a show, and, well... you know what happened. So, I'm gonna bring you a little sound like we play back in the bayous at The Swamp."

"Swamp Jesus! Pass the bucket and praise the Lord!" came the familiar voice of a regular from the back of the bar. Aubrey reached under the counter and handed the tip bucket into the crowd.

Dillon laughed and stroked his beard. He answered the heckler, "I've been called worse. Let's hit it, boys."

He turned to Billy. Billy's drumsticks clicked together as he counted the band in.

Dillon's voice trembled on the first few words, but he watched as the crowd leaned in and started swaying to the rhythm. A few people stood and danced beside their tables, and as the minutes passed, the dance floor filled.

This was the moment Dillon had been chasing. This was what he was meant to do. He felt it in his gut, his bones. Music wasn't his escape from where he started; it was his path forward. His way through.

The next morning, Dillon woke up on Greg's couch. The apartment was spotless; clearly, the maid had been by recently.

As he opened his eyes, Greg walked into the room and sat at the end of the sofa. Dillon sat up to make room.

Right away, Dillon noticed Greg wasn't smiling. That was rare. A wave of unease hit him hard.

Greg said, "My mom called me last night."

"Cool," Dillon replied. "How's she doing?"

"Ah, buddy..." Greg averted his eyes. "She's... okay."

A heavy silence settled between them.

Dread tightened in Dillon's chest. Greg never acted like this.

"It's your mom," Greg finally said, a tear sliding from the corner of his eye.

Panic chased out the fear building in Dillon's chest.

"What's wrong with my mom?" he asked, his voice cracking higher than he intended.

Greg's face twisted with grief as he fought to keep himself composed. He choked out the words, "There... there was a fire. The trailer..."

Shock surged through Dillon. He blinked hard, trying to convince himself this was real. His mind spun through possible explanations as Greg continued, tears streaming down his cheeks.

"They're not sure, but it looks like someone fell asleep smoking. My mom said one of her friends at the fire department told her the trailer was gone before they even got there."

Dillon stood and faced Greg, anger rising in his throat. "You don't know. She could be okay! How do they even know she was home?"

Greg looked up at him, pain in his eyes. He wiped his face and said as gently as he could, "They recovered your mom... and Devon. I'm so sorry, brother."

Dillon squeezed his eyes shut. His head pounded. He felt adrift, disconnected from reality. When he opened his eyes again, the room swam through a haze of tears. He tried to deny it. Tried to rationalize it away. But the words echoed in his head. Images flipped through his mind's eye: his mom sitting on the bathroom counter curling her hair, picking through junk on the roadside, sitting on the ratty couch in their living room listening to him play. He saw her smile, picking flowers on one of their walks.

His memory flashed to Devon's fat butt in the recliner, and arguments he'd had with Denise. He remembered

Denise sitting on Devon's lap at a bonfire. She was so happy that night. Maybe Devon hadn't been her worst choice.

He sat down slowly, elbows on his knees, and buried his face in his hands as the sobs took over. Greg sat quietly beside him.

After a long silence, Dillon leaned back and rubbed his eyes. A numbness rolled over him. He was so tired. Louisiana felt far away. Somewhere in his mind, his mother was there, still alive. He knew it wasn't true, but it felt true. At least, it felt like it could be true, if he wanted it hard enough.

He folded his hands in his lap and looked at Greg, who waited patiently.

"What now?" Dillon asked, hollow.

Greg answered gently, "I think we're going to have to make some arrangements."

Dillon stared at him, then replied in a flat tone, "I don't know how to do that."

"Haven't I always had your back? Since first grade, homie." Greg offered a small smile. "I'll call my parents back. They'll know what to do."

Dillon nodded mechanically, grateful Greg was there. Like Greg had said, he had always been there. When Dillon didn't have lunch money. When he was struggling to pass algebra. When he had a crush on Paige, what was her last name? She made fun of him, and Greg roasted her in front of their entire sixth-grade class. Dillon had no idea what Greg got out of their friendship, yet he was always there. Dillon imagined it must be what having a brother felt like. He just couldn't explain it any other way.

It took a few days for everything to be arranged. Dillon felt hollow, detached from the world. He knew, somewhere in that blurred time, Greg and his parents had handled the details.

Greg drove Dillon back for the funeral. Dillon didn't speak during the trip. He stared out the car window, lost in thought, as the landscape changed around him.

The rolling green hills of middle Tennessee gave way to the pine-lined highways of Mississippi, then to the wide-open fields and lazy waterways of Louisiana. Somewhere along the way, they stopped. They bought food at a convenience store. It wasn't how Dillon remembered it. The food was greasy and tasteless. The store was crammed with imported junk. There was no magic here, and Dillon didn't feel like he was home. He wanted to run back to the safety of Aubrey, Flumpy, and the saloon. He wanted to think about his future, not relive his past.

Greg pulled into the cemetery and parked on the grass behind a row of cars that had arrived earlier. Dillon stepped out into the heavy summer heat. He adjusted the dress jacket he'd borrowed for the occasion, though he still wore the same boots and jeans as always. His hair was tied neatly back in a ponytail, and his beard was combed. He took a pair of aviator sunglasses from his jacket pocket and pushed them onto his nose.

They walked toward the tent set up beside the open grave. Denise's casket gleamed in the sun. Her smile flashed through Dillon's mind as he found a folding chair and sat down. Greg followed silently behind.

Dillon noticed how few people had come. Was this the measure of his mother's life? Had she meant so little that only Greg's parents, Julio, and a handful of familiar acquaintances had shown up to say goodbye?

The minister smiled gently and offered his condolences as Dillon approached. He began to speak to the gathered mourners. Dillon heard the words but didn't absorb them. He could feel the heels of his boots sinking into the soft ground. The rites became background noise, a low hum behind the whirlwind of thoughts and memories flooding his mind. It had only been the two of them for so long. Sure, there had been the endless parade of boyfriends, but she tried to be a good mom. She loved him and told him so all the time. He remembered her saying, "I'm not everyone's cup of tea, but some people prefer a little whiskey."

A red cardinal landed on the casket. For just a moment, Dillon felt as if the bird were watching him. Then it lifted its wings and flew away.

CHAPTER SEVEN

DILLON RETURNED TO NASHVILLE and settled into a routine with the band. He watched in the mirror as his beard grew in, taking on a shaggier look. Sure, making music was work, but it was fun. He figured the others felt the same. They were all family men, playing for the thrill of live shows and holding onto their youthful dreams of being rock stars. They didn't mind him leading the group; they saw in him the same fire and hope they'd once had themselves. Lately, they laughed more. And Tyler, Tyler was a songwriter like no one Dillon had ever met. He had this bluesy sound that hit people deep.

Tyler even introduced Dillon to the pedal steel, a strange-looking console with strings, pedals, and knee levers that seemed more machine than instrument.

One afternoon, not long after Dillon quietly celebrated his twenty-first birthday, he showed up at the bar a little earlier than usual. A couple of day drinkers were hunched over the counter. A man and woman whispered and laughed at one of the floor tables. Two other guys sat apart, looking like they were in the middle of a late-afternoon business meeting.

Ashley was cutting fruit at the far end of the bar. Dillon glanced at the stage, where Bill was adjusting his drum kit. Bill paused long enough to give a short wave.

"Got new heads, wanted to break them in before tonight," Bill said, explaining without being asked.

Dillon waved back in acknowledgment and turned to Aubrey.

"Hey, cowboy," she said with a smile.

Dillon grinned. He dug into his pocket and pulled out a keychain. It was attached to an oblong piece of white rubber printed with a palm tree and the words: Isle of

Capri Casino, Vicksburg, in colorful font. He handed it to Aubrey.

She tried not to laugh at the absurd little souvenir from her hometown. Dillon felt a wave of embarrassment, but she caught it quickly and said gently, "You were so sweet to think about me. Thank you."

Dillon was just starting to think of what to say next when Boone burst through the door. He strode up to Aubrey and barked, "Why don't you make me a drink and tell Flumpy I want to talk to him?"

Aubrey looked him dead in the eye. "I'm pretty sure you're done here."

Boone laughed. "We'll see. Now get that pretty little caboose moving and bring me that drink."

Dillon turned to face him. Boone glanced over and scoffed. "What are you doing here during the day? Did they promote you to janitor? Sounds about right for a no-talent slug like you."

Dillon leaned against the bar. "Seems like this slug is the new front man. The position opened up after the last guy fell down on the job. I guess you could call it a battlefield promotion."

Boone flushed and spun to face him. Just then, Flumpy appeared beside Aubrey.

"What do you need, Boone?"

Boone swallowed and turned toward Flumpy. His demeanor softened. "I was hoping we could talk. Maybe just the two of us."

Flumpy crossed his arms. "I don't think we have anything to discuss."

Boone coughed and stared down at his shoes before lifting his eyes. "I wasn't planning a team meeting, but I can adjust. I know I messed up. It won't happen again."

Flumpy stood firm. "I don't think so, Boone. You're not drawing the crowds anymore, and frankly, you're more trouble than you're worth."

Desperation washed over Boone's face. He looked older. His voice turned pleading. "Flumpy, you can't do this to me. I'm the one who put this place on the map. I brought in the crowds. Do you know how competitive it is out there? This town is full of no-talent wannabes who'll play for free just to be heard. Man, I've got bills to pay and I haven't landed a single paying gig since I left."

Flumpy's eyes softened, though his stance didn't change. His voice was calm. "We're done, Boone. I appreciate what you did back in the day, but that was then. Now it's over."

Boone tensed, gritting his teeth. "This is wrong and you know it. I'll be back." As he turned, he caught sight of Dillon still standing nearby. He spat, "And you, I see you trying to get in Aubrey's pants. Let me save you some time. She's not worth it."

Heat surged through Dillon's body. In a flash, his fist connected with Boone's nose. Blood burst from Boone's face. He clutched his nose and shouted to Aubrey, "Give me a damn towel!"

Aubrey tossed him a dirty bar rag. Boone caught it and pressed it to his face.

"What's wrong with you?" he snapped at Dillon. "I have to make a living with this face." He tilted his head back to slow the bleeding, pinching his nose as he shuffled toward the door. "Flumpy, this bar would be nothing without me. It will be nothing! They came to see me, not you."

"You'll regret this," he muttered before disappearing outside.

Dillon watched him go, rubbing his aching hand with the other. The punch had landed solidly, and the dull throb lingered as a reminder. Flumpy stared at him. Dillon dropped his head.

"I'm sorry," he said.

"Sorry?" Flumpy raised an eyebrow. "I just want to thank you for taking out the trash." A faint grin curled at the edges of his mouth. "Listen, kid, he's been spiraling for a long time. I knew it'd come to this, either he moves on or we both go down the same drain. Don't let my hesitation to cut bait hold you back."

Dillon let the silence between them swell with the weight of the moment. A part of him wondered if he'd gone too far, if there was something about Boone he wasn't seeing. He didn't know how to respond to someone giving him hope. His mom had. Arthur had. They were gone. Now, Flumpy was talking.

"It was a long time coming," Flumpy said. "My dad used to say there's a fine line between giving a hand up and giving a handout. Do me a favor, don't prove I can make the same mistake twice."

As Flumpy walked away, Dillon noticed Aubrey watching him. His face flushed. Was this going to be his future? He wanted to make it, to be known and successful for his music. But so had Boone. He didn't know how he'd do it, but he was sure of one thing: he wasn't going down that same path.

He looked up again. Aubrey was still watching. She held his gaze for a moment, then returned to cutting fruit, focusing intently on her task. A small smile played on her lips, like she was trying not to let it show.

Dillon didn't let the moment pass.

"I guess this would be a bad time to ask you to dinner or something." He could hear the nervousness in his voice. He wondered if she could, too.

She didn't stop slicing. Without looking at him or changing her tone, she said, "Yep, bad time to be doing that."

Silence settled between them. Dillon turned toward the stage and started walking.

"My place. Seven o'clock Monday night," Aubrey said. "I'll cook. Bring wine. And not the cheap crap in a box."

Dillon was elated. He forced himself not to turn back and gush over the prospect of having dinner with her. "Yes, ma'am. No wine in a box."

The next few days passed quickly. Dillon wanted to be at work as much as possible. Every minute there meant being close to Aubrey, and their connection felt easy. They laughed about everything and nothing. He learned she'd left home after her dad died of a sudden heart attack. She didn't see much of a future in Vicksburg beyond marrying a farmer or someone who worked the river barges.

She had a pretty big family, traditional Southern, large, and complicated, as she put it.

In the bigger picture, Tyler pushed him differently than Arthur had. It felt more like collaboration. Bill described it as "finding your sound." Arthur had said, "Give the music space." Dillon began to believe there might be a path for him. He hadn't come to Nashville chasing fame, or maybe he had and just didn't know it at the time.

It felt like it took a month for Monday to arrive. Aubrey had teased him every day. He was pretty sure she was just as excited as he was. Dillon asked the clerk at a corner liquor store for the best wine to pair with dinner.

The old man behind the counter looked confused. He scratched his chin and glanced around the store, like he was seeing it for the first time, even though he'd been there for decades.

"I don't get that question," he finally said.

Dillon laughed softly. "Not often, huh?"

The clerk's eyes twinkled. "Ever!"

He left his stool behind the register and walked over to a wall lined with bottles. After scanning the shelves, he selected a dusty one and wiped it clean with the palm of his hand. Turning to Dillon, he said, "This is a red wine from California. I hear Napa Valley makes some good ones."

Dillon took the bottle and examined the label, but the information meant nothing to him. He shrugged. "Okay."

He followed the clerk back to the register.

The clerk rang it up, bagged the bottle, and stopped Dillon just as he was about to leave.

"Wait."

The man reached into a box at the end of the counter and pulled out a corkscrew, handing it to Dillon. "You'll need this gadget to open the bottle. I figure if the top doesn't screw off, it must be a better choice."

Dillon nodded and thanked him, slipping the corkscrew into his pocket. He gave a small wave as he left the store.

The walk to Aubrey's house wasn't far. The tall buildings of downtown faded behind him as the streets turned residential. The yards were small, with cars wedged into every available space. Most of the homes were weathered red or brown brick, many with porches outfitted with swings and chairs for watching the world go by.

Wooden trim, painted white, soft blue, or tan, had faded under the weight of Southern summers and winters. Though Dillon was used to much less congestion, he felt an unexpected comfort in the neighborhood's quiet, lived-in charm. A bicycle left in a front yard or a car hood propped open with a man tinkering beneath it added to the sense of welcome.

Dillon's heart raced as he walked. He ran his hands down the starched white shirt he wore. Greg had ironed it for him. Dillon figured he shouldn't be surprised that Greg could iron. That "always neatly dressed" habit came from his mother. It was just one more gesture of care from Greg that Dillon couldn't quite explain.

Greg had always been there to help him. He'd once put it this way: "I see it like this, blood isn't family. Family is who you choose and who chooses you, in good times and bad. You're either family or you're not. Plus, you're an investment. When you're a famous performer standing under those bright lights, it'll be your turn to buy."

Dillon had thought about that statement many times. He'd quietly vowed to reward Greg over and over. Until recently, he couldn't remember a time when he truly believed being famous was something he could do. But Greg had been telling him it was his future for most of their lives.

He spotted the house number Aubrey had given him. Her place didn't stand out from the others. The yard was worn, with a cracked concrete walkway leading to two black metal security doors at the top of four steps. It was a multi-family home. The porch was wide, decorated with potted plants and white wicker furniture.

His palms were damp as he shifted the wine bottle from one hand to the other and knocked on the door. His imagination raced with images of Aubrey, her smile, her easy way of handling anything that came her way. He'd seen her nearly every day for the past week, and now he felt nervous about what he'd say. For a moment, he wondered if she liked him, or had he misread the whole situation? Could she be thinking they were just friends having dinner?

Aubrey answered after a few seconds, smiling as she invited him in. Dillon wasn't sure what he'd expected, but it wasn't this. He felt like he was stepping into another world as he crossed the threshold. Sunlight poured through large windows and danced across polished wood floors. The high ceilings were trimmed with white, intricately scrolled molding. The space wasn't extravagant, but it was vibrant and full of cheerful color.

The trinkets on the shelves and mantel seemed thoughtfully placed, giving the space a warm, curated feel. It wasn't magazine-perfect, but it was tasteful and inviting. More than seeing it, Dillon felt that the home had been built with care.

Aubrey gave him a moment to take it all in. It was clear she was proud of what she'd made.

"Come on back to the kitchen. Dinner's on the stove," she said, taking the wine bottle from his hands and leading the way.

He noticed the sway in her hips was a little more exaggerated than usual, or was he imagining that too?

He followed her down a narrow hallway. As they passed a bedroom, he peeked in, and it matched the style and energy of the living room.

At the end of the hallway, they stepped into a large room with a dining set in one corner and a small kitchenette along the back wall. Cabinets lined the space, interrupted only by a fridge, sink, and gas stove. Pots and pans bubbled and hissed, releasing rich smells that reminded Dillon just how hungry he was.

Aubrey pulled the wine from the bag and studied the label, her lips pursed as she read. Dillon suddenly worried he'd made a bad choice.

But then she looked at him with a teasing smile. "This'll be perfect. Let me grab my wine opener."

Dillon fumbled in his pocket and pulled out a corkscrew. "I've got one right here."

"Oh," she said, "you came prepared. Want to open it?"

He blushed. "I, uh... why don't you?"

She took the corkscrew from his hand and opened the bottle with practiced ease. "Look in the cabinet at the end. Get us two glasses."

Dillon opened the cabinet and froze at the array of glassware.

"Two of the long-stemmed ones on the top shelf will do," Aubrey said helpfully.

He turned with the glasses, and she filled each halfway. She took a sip and set her glass on the table.

"Come sit," she said. "I'll serve dinner."

Dillon settled into a chair while she plated creamy mushrooms and pork medallions.

"Oh my god," he said after the first bite. "This is delicious. Where'd you learn to cook like this?"

Aubrey sat and picked at her food. "Pork Marsala. I dated this guy, Brad, for a while. It was his go-to dish. I think he cooked it for every girl he ever dated."

Dillon leaned back in his chair and took another sip of wine, watching the red liquid swirl around the glass. "I don't think I've ever said I was glad a girl I like had dated someone else, but Brad, thanks, buddy."

She laughed softly. "Let's just say he was a hell of a cook. It usually got him what he wanted."

She tilted her head, smiling. "Is that what's happening? You're seeing me?"

Dillon leaned in, steady and sure. He couldn't deny how much he wanted her. A flicker of doubt gripped his chest. What if he'd misread all the signs? Embarrassment loomed, but he couldn't stop himself.

"I sure hope so," he said.

Aubrey pushed her plate aside and leaned toward him. Dillon set his glass down and met her halfway for their first kiss.

He woke the next morning to the sound of rain. Aubrey lay beside him, her hair tousled across the pillow. Sitting up, he watched water slide down the windowpane. In the corner of the room, a battered, scratched guitar caught his eye.

Moving quietly, he got out of bed and crossed the room to retrieve it. As he picked it up to admire it, she spoke behind him.

"It was my dad's. He loved playing it."

He turned to her. "Do you mind?"

She shook her head.

He brought the guitar back to the bed and sat on the edge while she watched. He strummed a few chords and shifted to see her better.

Aubrey adjusted the pillows behind her and sat up straight. She watched dreamily as Dillon caressed her father's guitar. Speaking as if from a faraway place, she said,

"My dad worked at a shoe factory over in Clarksville. He spent 35 years there. They made soles."

Dillon paused to listen as she reminisced.

"He never said he hated his job. At least not to me. Almost every weekend, Mom cooked these big Sunday dinners. We never knew who'd show up to eat. Dad always said if the front door was open, you were invited. Nearly every Sunday afternoon, he and his beer-drinking buddies from the factory would end up on the deck in the backyard, playing music."

She looked at Dillon, her eyes still distant. "It was a great way to grow up."

"I've got this song stuck in my head," he said. "Tell me what you think."

Dillon cleared his throat and began to sing:

"I have roamed the streets called memory.

I have swum through the blood in my veins.

I have stared into the heart of the sun,

But I have never met a woman like you..."

Aubrey listened, captivated, while the rain tapped a soft rhythm to his song.

Chapter Eight

Dillon showed up at the bar at his usual time, surprised by how packed it was. He had to walk past a line just to get through the front door. Flumpy gave him a nod and kept checking IDs.

Dillon scanned the room for Aubrey. She paused from taking an order just long enough to flash him a smile. He felt something unfamiliar. It was hard to define at first, but the only word that came to mind was complete.

He pushed through the crowd with his guitar case until he reached the stage.

Bill was busy adjusting his kit. Blake was already tuning his guitar. Tyler met Dillon the moment both of his feet hit the stage.

"What's up?" Tyler asked.

Dillon acknowledged his bandmate with a nod. "Hey, man. Are you ready to go?"

"For sure," Tyler replied. "I've got a new song I want us to try."

"Really? Now? We're about to go on."

"Yeah, I know. But this is the only time I've seen you. I want to try it out."

Dillon didn't like being put on the spot, but he understood Tyler had a point.

"Okay," he finally said. "Get the guys on the same page, and let's give it a shot."

Tyler handed him a sheet with the lyrics and turned toward the others. Dillon watched them huddle together, working out the details of the song. He looked down at the page and began mouthing the words under his breath. After going through them a couple of times, he turned to face the crowd.

The stage lights made it hard to see clearly, but he stroked his beard and studied the patrons. Everyone looked like they were having a good time. He tried to catch Aubrey's eye again, but she was too busy slinging drinks.

Somewhere in the crowd, someone shouted, "Swamp Jesus!"

Dillon grinned and leaned into the mic.

"That's right. We're about to bring you some down-home, born-on-the-bayou, raised-in-the-black-water music that'll make you want to dance, sing, and maybe even fall in love, all at once."

"Woo!" and "Hell yeah!" echoed from different parts of the room, rising above the murmur of the crowd.

"We're starting with something a little different tonight," he told the audience. "My friend and axeman, Tyler, wrote this one, and you're gonna be the first to hear it. Are you ready?!"

Dillon glanced at the lyrics one last time, turned to check that the others were ready, and signaled Bill to count them in. The first note rang out, long and loud, as Tyler slid a metal ring across the strings of his guitar. Blake stepped up with his harmonica in hand. Blues met rock met country as the notes tangled together. Bill dropped the beat, and Dillon's heart lifted as he watched excitement ripple through the crowd.

He leaned into the microphone and cleared his throat. There was a thrill, a touch of danger, as he began to sing. He felt the spark of electricity and a flicker of fear as he placed his trust in Tyler. He scanned the words and eased into the opening chorus: "She used to be my cherry red..."

Dillon sang with a passion that fed the crowd. If there was a perfect storm for him, this was it.

The band's energy was matched by the crowd all night. As the first set closed, Dillon noticed Greg leaning against the bar. He stood out among the people around him, not just because of his height, but because of his semi-formal style: a golf shirt, slacks, and comfortable shoes. He was an island in a sea of country-western energy. The Brendas were with him, dancing, hollering, and partying to the music. They had fully embraced the scene in matching pink cowboy boots, fringed midriff jackets, and western hats.

Dillon approached Greg and gave him a brotherly hug.

"What are you doing here?" Dillon asked.

Greg smiled. "We party all the time at the apartments, and I figured I should get out and support my buddy. Plus, the maid came today, and my parents are visiting tomorrow."

"Ah, gotta keep the place clean. I see," Dillon laughed.

Greg added conspiratorially, "Also, they don't know you're living there."

Dillon nodded. "No worries. I think I can crash at Aubrey's. I'll ask her later."

Flumpy interrupted their conversation. "Dillon, there's someone I want you to meet."

Brenda Gayle stepped up beside him. "Hello there, big guy. Should you know me?"

Flumpy gave her a gruff look and muttered, "Funny. Probably not. You look closer to high school than having a job."

Brenda Gayle stepped in close and said, "Considering I start my residency next year, you may be right."

Flumpy tried to hide a half-smile. "A smart girl. I like that. But right now, I need to introduce these two."

Brenda Gayle winked at him and turned back to chat with Brenda Jean. Dillon noticed Flumpy blush.

Flumpy turned to him. "Dillon, this is John Reins. He's a friend of mine in the music business."

The man who stepped forward to shake Dillon's hand wasn't what he expected. Neatly dressed in slacks and a starched plaid shirt, he looked more like a Sears catalog model than a music agent.

"Hi, Dillon. Good to meet you," John said. "Flumpy told me I might want to come hear you play."

"Well, thank you, John," Dillon replied, shaking his hand.

Flumpy placed a hand on John's shoulder as he addressed Dillon. "He's the real deal, boy. Don't take this lightly."

Dillon glanced between the two men. "Of course not. I hope you're here to enjoy the show, John."

John smiled to himself and answered coolly, "I'm staying. Flumpy isn't one to brag or waste anyone's time.

He said some promising things about you, and frankly, it's hard to stand out in this city. Let's just say it helps to know someone in the business."

"Oh," John added, producing a business card, "in case I leave before your set is over, here's my information. Maybe we can talk sometime."

Dillon placed his thumbs in his pockets and stepped back. "I guess we can talk. About what, exactly?"

John flashed a million-dollar grin, showing off perfect white teeth. "You know, your goals, your plans for the future. That kind of thing. What's your story?"

Dillon nodded. "Okay, I appreciate it. I've got to get back on stage now. Hope you like what you hear. The band is off the hook, if I say so myself."

As an afterthought, Dillon added, "John?"

John looked at him expectantly.

Dillon continued, "I've been promised things before, and..."

John cut him off. "I'm not here to guarantee you anything. I'm here because Flumpy put you on my radar. I'll be here to enjoy the show. Let's talk soon. Break a leg."

He headed toward the stage, then turned briefly to see John settling into a chair with a good view.

Dillon felt a knot forming in his stomach. He'd performed onstage more times than he could count, but this felt different. John could change his life. Dillon imagined all the good he could do, how much better life could be for the people around him... If he didn't mess it up.

Brenda Gayle smiled as Flumpy chatted with her. Was Flumpy full-on grinning?

Dillon had a sense that anything could happen tonight. Then, a sudden wave of foreboding swept through him.

He scanned the crowd, realizing he was looking for Boone.

That made no sense. Why would Boone be here?

The feeling passed just as quickly as it came, and Dillon felt silly for even thinking about Boone. Everything was finally going his way. Surely Boone had moved on.

Dillon leaned into the microphone and began to sing.

His voice cracked. A high-pitched squeak escaped his throat. Embarrassed, he stopped. Silence.

He glanced in John's direction. John calmly watched the stage, his expression unreadable. Whatever he was thinking, he didn't show it.

Dillon turned back to the band, who had also stopped.

He smiled. "Let's try that again, boys."

Bill started the beat. Blake eased into the rhythm. Tyler picked up the lead.

Dillon brought home the opening lines.

Lost in a world where he stood on center stage, Dillon sang like no one was watching.

The night finally wound down. Dillon felt good.

The band was tired but upbeat. Bill slipped his drumsticks into his back pocket. Tyler and Blake coiled cords and packed away instruments.

People lingered at the bar, then slowly filtered out past Flumpy at the door.

Aubrey gave Dillon a flirtatious look as she wiped the counter with a bar towel. He leaned against it, watching her.

He asked hesitantly, "Greg needs me to stay out of the house tonight. Would you mind if I stayed with you?"

Aubrey raised a hand like a fan and used an exaggerated Southern belle accent. "Lordy, sir, you are certainly forward. How can a lady be expected to have an unattached young man at her house overnight, no less?"

Dillon leaned a little farther over the counter and said playfully, "Maybe you could make me attached."

Aubrey didn't answer. She gave him a flirty glance as she walked to the other end of the bar.

He woke the next morning in her bed. The soft, warm sheets pulled him back toward dreamland, but the smell of bacon lured him awake. He blinked away sleep and got up, stretching as he looked around the room. Was it biscuits, he smelled too? Scratching the band of his boxers, Dillon padded toward the kitchen.

Aubrey stood at the stove, her back to him, busy cooking. She wore a light blue kimono that fell just to her knees. Dillon stepped in close, his chest brushing against her back. He ran his fingertips along her thighs and up to her hips.

"Good morning," she said, not turning around.

"It smells amazing in here," he murmured, pressing a kiss to the nape of her neck.

She laughed and gave him a playful push. "If you don't stop, your breakfast's going to burn."

Dillon moved to the cabinet and pulled out plates and glasses. "Thanks for letting me stay last night."

Aubrey turned off the burner and removed a pan from the heat. Facing him now, she grinned. "Oh, you owe me, boy."

She plated the food and carried it to the table while Dillon poured orange juice into two glasses. As they sat down to eat, Aubrey pointed her fork at him.

"So, what's your plan?"

Dillon hesitated. "John asked me the same thing last night. What do you mean?"

"Is floating between Greg's couch and my bed... your life plan?"

Dillon grinned. "Well, I like the floating-in-your-bed part."

"What if you didn't have to float?" she asked softly. When she looked up, Dillon saw something vulnerable in her eyes. "You could stay here."

He smiled. "Are you asking me to move in?"

"Not if you prefer Greg's couch."

Aubrey looked down at her plate. A few seconds passed, and the silence between them grew heavier. Dillon questioned his motives. Was this just a matter of convenience, or was it truly what he wanted? He liked the idea of waking up every day in Aubrey's cozy bed. He was feeling something for her, something deeper than anything he'd felt before. Most of all, he trusted her.

Aubrey laughed. "Sometimes you're so dumb. Wait, who's John?"

Dillon thought, "She always knows what she wants." He answered, "Some agent Flumpy introduced me to. Do you know him?"

"No, but Flumpy knows everyone in town. You should call him."

She rose from the table and walked over to where Dillon sat. He slid his chair back, and she eased onto his lap, wrapping her arms around his neck.

"Now that you live here, you should know, there are a few rules," she said, her voice playful.

Dillon gazed up at her dreamily. "Yeah? What are they?"

"Well, really just two." She leaned in closer. "Whoever doesn't cook has to clean the kitchen."

"Uh-huh," he murmured.

"And sing to me. Every day. I hear you can sing."

"Uh-huh," he said again, closing the space between them with a kiss. Dillon wasn't sure how he'd ended up here, this moment, this life, and he wondered: could it get any better, or would it even last?

Chapter Nine

The night was busy. The crowd had picked up. Dillon stroked his full beard and looked out from the stage at the room full of guests. Flumpy stood at the door, chatting with people as they entered. A new doorman sat on a stool beside him, collecting cover charges. Johnny zipped between customers, moving carefully to avoid spilling drinks or bumping into anyone. Aubrey was busy behind the bar, while a new bartender worked the opposite end. Greg and the Brendas sat at a table with several other college students, drinking beer and having fun.

Tyler tapped Dillon on the shoulder and pointed toward the door. "What do you think is going on there?" he asked.

Dillon followed his gaze and saw Boone talking to Flumpy. Boone wore a long trench coat that ended just above his boots, and his cowboy hat was tilted back from his face. He looked tired. Dillon couldn't hear what they were saying. Boone waved his arms dramatically, as if trying to make a point Flumpy wasn't interested in hearing.

Dillon turned back to Tyler. "I don't know, but it sure seems like trouble whenever he shows up."

Flumpy looked concerned as Boone walked away and headed for the bar. He made his way to the far end, where the new bartender was working. Dillon watched as Boone ordered, and the bartender poured water into a glass from the soda gun. Then Dillon shifted his focus back to entertaining the crowd.

He kept an eye on Boone as the band performed. Boone lingered near the bar, barely speaking to anyone. He watched song after song like it was a private performance.

His expression showed defeat or maybe deep sadness. Dillon was reminded of a time when his mother brought home a puppy, and her then-boyfriend told her she couldn't keep "another mouth to feed." The boyfriend had left the trailer with the puppy under his arm. Minutes later, Dillon and his mother heard a single gunshot. His mother had worn the same look Boone wore now.

As the night went on, Dillon noticed Boone had drifted farther down the bar. He wasn't being loud or drawing attention to himself. If anything, he seemed completely absorbed in the show.

When Dillon came to a break, he stepped off the stage. Boone slipped past him and climbed behind the microphone. Dillon turned to stop him, but Boone was already there. He grabbed the mic. Most people didn't notice until he spoke.

"Good evening, everyone. I'm Boone Kane, and I have to make this quick."

A few people turned to look. The rest ignored him.

"Attention," he said louder this time, his voice cracking slightly as it rose.

Then he dropped his hand beneath his coat and pulled out a six-shooter.

Time stood still. Is that a real gun? Dillon thought. He glanced across the bar. Some people were sliding from their chairs to the floor. The new bartender ducked behind the bar. Aubrey stood frozen, staring at Boone. One guy ran out the front door, phone held to his ear.

Tyler grabbed Bill's arm and guided him off the stage as quietly as he could. Blake ducked behind the riser on the opposite side. Boone raised the weapon and fired into the ceiling. The shot cracked through the bar, silencing the room. All eyes turned to him.

"Okay," Boone said, "I'm sorry about that. I just need you to listen for a minute."

He lowered the gun slightly and paused to collect his thoughts.

"You see, I used to work here. I was the singer." He looked at Dillon, then turned to the crowd. "Flumpy, I'm the one they came to see. I brought in the crowd."

Sadness swept across his face.

"Maybe I drank a little too much. Yeah, I had a good time," he said, voice rising. "But I am the star."

Flumpy walked cautiously toward the stage. The stunned patrons parted to let him pass. Boone kept his eyes locked on him. When Flumpy was a few feet away, Boone raised the gun.

"You didn't have to let me go like that. I was loyal."

Flumpy raised his hands halfway. "Boone, we can work this out."

Boone began to cry. "I wish we could. But there's nothing out there for me. I'm sleeping in my damn car, Flumpy! In my damn car!"

Flumpy took another step. "It's going to be okay. Come on down and hand me that gun."

Boone stiffened. Tears streamed down his face. "Flumpy, I didn't mean for anything to get out of hand. I wanted what we all want when we come here. I came to Nashville with nothing, and that's how I'll leave."

Sirens wailed in the distance.

Boone leveled the gun at Flumpy. Flumpy raised his hands in vain to stop what he knew was coming.

Dillon saw the muzzle flash. Time seemed to slow. Flumpy fell backward, crashing through a table. Screams erupted as people scrambled. Flumpy didn't move.

Suddenly, time rushed forward again, as if struggling to keep pace. Boone raised the revolver to his temple. Police burst through the front doors. Boone wiped his face, then turned toward the approaching officers. Dillon watched as Boone squeezed the trigger.

This shot sounded louder than the first.

Dillon's ears rang as Boone crumpled to the floor. It wasn't dramatic. It certainly wasn't like anything Dillon had seen in the movies. Boone's body didn't twitch, and there was nothing heroic or poetic about what Dillon witnessed. Boone had fully captured the crowd's attention, possibly for the first time in his life, and that moment would stay with Dillon forever. All the bravado, the condescension, the drunken misogyny had led to this. Boone lay still, almost in defiance of the chaos he'd created. He had gotten the last word.

Dillon stood frozen in the horror he'd just seen.

Police swarmed the room. Two paramedics knelt beside Flumpy.

Someone spoke to him, it was an officer, but Dillon stared blankly. The words didn't register.

The next morning, Dillon woke in the chair he'd slept in. Aubrey stood beside him, handing him a cup of coffee. He sat up and glanced down the hospital corridor. Taking the white Styrofoam cup in both hands, he let the heat soak into his palms.

A nurse stepped into the hallway and said, "You can come in now."

Dillon and Aubrey walked into the room she had indicated. His hands trembled, memories of the previous night still raw, the weight of knowing his champion had nearly died sinking in. It could've just as easily been him that Boone shot. Aubrey gave his arm a reassuring squeeze as they entered. Dillon could see she was trying to be brave, but the strain showed in her eyes; she was just as shaken as he was.

Flumpy sat up in bed, looking irritated as he pushed food around on the tray in front of him. He glanced toward the door as they entered.

"I see getting shot didn't ruin your appetite," Aubrey teased.

Flumpy replied gruffly, "Maybe if they brought me some real food. Tell me you snuck in some Fat Mo's, and we'll be square."

Brenda Gayle walked into the room, her hair pulled into a neat bun, a doctor's smock buttoned over her clothes. She carried herself with calm authority.

"How's my little wounded warrior?" she asked, glancing at the clipboard in her hands.

Flumpy tried to hold back a grin, but the corners of his mouth betrayed him. "I'm ready to go home."

"Wait a minute, you're a doctor?" Dillon asked, surprised.

"Not yet," Brenda Gayle said, turning toward him. "Third-year intern. I added Grumpy Flumpy to my rounds so I can keep an eye on him."

"She's trying to get a peek at my johnson," Flumpy muttered.

Aubrey snickered.

Brenda Gayle stared at him evenly. "What makes you think I didn't peek while you were unconscious?"

Flumpy blushed and picked up a single-serving container of orange gelatin. He tried to sound cocky, but it didn't quite land.

"I bet you did. It'd be unforgettable... for you."

"Yeah, okay," Brenda Gayle said, rolling her eyes. "And you know I can't let you out of here yet. That has to come from your primary. According to your chart, you'll be under observation for three days."

"Where did you get shot?" Dillon asked, trying to steer the conversation elsewhere.

Flumpy tapped his right side. "Almost got me in the liver. The doctor said one inch lower, and I'd be a dead man."

He dipped his index finger into the gelatin, swirled it along the edge of the cup, then tossed the container back like a shot of liquor.

Brenda Gayle turned to the visitors. "He'll be fine. He just needs some rest. We want to make sure there are no complications." She glanced at Flumpy. "You, sir, are lucky it didn't hit any vital organs."

She scribbled a note on the chart and let it fall to her side. "Well, I've got patients to see. I'll catch y'all later."

Dillon and Aubrey said their goodbyes as Brenda Gayle left the room. John Reins passed her on his way in.

"Look at this!" John exclaimed. "Superman here can't be stopped by a speeding bullet."

Flumpy set the empty container back on the tray. "Everyone's a comedian today."

John shook hands with Dillon and Aubrey before turning to Flumpy. "My mother would say you were born under a lucky star."

Flumpy looked around the room self-consciously.

"I suppose," he said, not fully committing. "If the star ripped through your side and took half your innards with it. It hurts like heck."

A nurse entered and said, "Time to take his vitals and get him cleaned up. I hate to ask you to leave, but you can wait in the hall if you'd like."

Aubrey took Dillon's arm. "We have to go anyway. I've got inventory at the bar." She teased Flumpy, "Some of us have to work, while others just lie around all day."

Flumpy responded with an exaggerated eye roll.

"I'll walk out with you, if that's okay," John said to Dillon.

Dillon nodded and stepped closer to the bed. Lowering his voice slightly, he said to Flumpy, "I'll see you later. Let me know if you need anything."

Flumpy looked a little embarrassed by the attention and barked, "There's no reason to worry about me. I'm tough as rattlesnake hide and too mean to die."

Dillon patted his shoulder and walked out of the room with the other two visitors.

As they exited the elevator, John signaled for Dillon to stop. He stepped into Dillon's personal space and spoke in calm, even tones. "You haven't called me to set up a meeting."

"Yeah, I know," Dillon said. "I got busy and"

John cut him off. "I very rarely give a musician a second chance if they blow me off. Dillon, I think you've got something special. Let's have lunch on Wednesday. We'll meet at Puckett's at eleven."

Dillon shook his hand. "I'll see you there."

The next few months passed in a blur. Lunch with John turned into studio time, meetings with other record execs, rehearsals with the band, and writing sessions with Tyler. Dillon was swept up in the whirlwind of working with John's firm and in his time with Aubrey. She was always there, encouraging him, and when he held her, nothing else mattered.

Nights at the bar had mostly returned to normal. Flumpy had attached a small nameplate dedicated to Boone at the end of the bar. Every evening, he quietly filled a rocks glass with water and placed it beside the memorial. He knew he couldn't have saved Boone, and he wasn't angry about being shot. What stayed with him was the sadness of watching his talented friend's long spiral come to such an end. He paid homage in the best way he knew how.

People filled the building to watch Dillon onstage, and Flumpy hired more staff. Happiness was the only word Dillon could find to describe how he felt. It had been foreign at first, now, it was what he craved.

Then the day came. Dillon looked in the mirror one last time. He adjusted his turquoise jacket and shifted to view himself from different angles. He studied his face, pushed his hair back, and stroked his long beard, taking in the whole package. His mom would've loved to see this moment. Arthur's voice echoed in his mind: "Play with intention. Let the music go where it wants, then take a break. Leave space."

Satisfied, he carefully placed a cowboy hat on his head and turned to walk through the dressing room door.

He made his way down a long hallway. Some people stood chatting, others rushed past on missions he couldn't guess. He passed stacks of stage equipment, lighting rigs, and towering boxes. Turning a corner, he saw Greg, Aubrey, and John standing together.

Greg patted him on the shoulder. "I'm proud of you, brother."

Aubrey threw her arms around his neck and hugged him tightly. She whispered, "I knew you could do it."

Dillon pulled back just enough to meet her eyes. "I love you," he said.

Aubrey's eyes sparkled. She stroked his cheek and ran her fingers down his beard. "I love you, too."

He released her and turned to John. John took his hand. The two men locked eyes for a long moment.

"I believe in you," John said simply.

Dillon nodded. He let go of John's hand and stepped toward the large black curtain at the end of the hallway. He took a deep breath, closed his eyes, and murmured, "I love you, Mom."

Then he stepped through the curtain.

A loud din greeted him. He walked toward the sound, eyes lowered to the scarred black floor. The noise sharpened into a chant: "Swamp Jesus. Swamp Jesus."

As Dillon stepped onto the stage, the chanting swelled. He looked out but couldn't see the crowd through the glare of the stage lights. He picked up a guitar from a nearby stand and slung the strap over his neck. Leaning into the mic, he waited as the lights dimmed just enough to reveal thousands of faces staring back. Yellow buckets flew back and forth across the crowd. Toward the back of the hall, a massive banner read: Grand Ole Opry.

Dillon smiled and spoke into the mic. "Thank you, Nashville. It's time to party Louisiana style."

The crowd roared, still chanting. Dillon strummed his guitar and began to sing:

"Well, take me back to the Tennessee Valley,

Where there's love on the corner and peace in the alley.

Ah, Mississippi River, don't you come my way..."

About the Author

Writing has been a passion for Scott since his teen years, yet he didn't find a chance to publicly apply his skills until he wrote his first children's book, Tiger at the Table (2003) This was a story about teaching children table manners on an imaginative level they could understand. That book opened the door for many projects that followed. His second children's book, Shiloh Just Right (2004), was the story of self esteem for children and preempted the

Spanish version of his first book, Tigre a la Mesa (2005). After being approached by a representative from his local library association, Scott partnered with Linda Higgins and Arcadia Press to write a pictorial history of his place of birth, Images of Madison County, (2009).

Scott took the offer from a long time friend and publisher to write as a food columnist for two magazines under Harvey Boyd's stewardship, Good Ol' Boys and Hey Y'all.

Scott was involved with many projects that took him away from writing though he enjoyed his time in front of the camera as host of Guys Cook Too and Taking A Cooking Adventure. Scott relocated to Florida near the beginning of the pandemic, which led to Scott being the host of podcast, Dying To Eat. He released Biloxi, A Story of Hope,(Jan 2025) to bring light in a historical fiction atmosphere to systemic racism. Biloxi was presented as an award winner in August from Florida Writers' and Publishers' Association.

This book, Swamp Jesus, (Aug 2025) is a fictional tale of a young man that works to beat the odds and follow his dreams to escape a life of poverty in Louisiana. The protagonist, Dillon, has one skill he can rely, playing guitar. Where better to seek success than Nashville, home of country music?

If you would like to contact Scott, write readscottsbooks@gmail.com.